Acting Edition

Somewhere Over the Border

by Brian Quijada

Co-Orchestrations by
Yendrys Cespedes and Julián Mesri

Co-Vocal Arrangements by
Julián Mesri and Brian Quijada

FOR PRODUCTION INQUIRIES

UNITED STATES AND CANADA
info@concordtheatricals.com
1-866-979-0447

UNITED KINGDOM AND EUROPE
licensing@concordtheatricals.co.uk
020-7054-7298

Each title is subject to availability from Concord Theatricals Corp., depending upon country of performance. Please be aware that *SOMEWHERE OVER THE BORDER* may not be licensed by Concord Theatricals Corp. in your territory. Professional and amateur producers should contact the nearest Concord Theatricals Corp. office or licensing partner to verify availability.

No one shall make any changes in this title(s) for the purpose of production. No part of this book may be reproduced, stored in a retrieval system, scanned, uploaded, or transmitted in any form, by any means, now known or yet to be invented, including mechanical, electronic, digital, photocopying, recording, videotaping, or otherwise, without the prior written permission of the publisher. No one shall share this title(s), or any part of this title(s), through any social media or file hosting websites.

For all inquiries regarding motion picture, television, online /digital and other media rights, please contact Concord Theatricals Corp.

THIRD-PARTY MATERIALS USE NOTE

Licensees are solely responsible for obtaining formal written permission from copyright owners to use copyrighted third-party materials (e.g., incidental music not provided in connection with a performance license, artworks, logos) in the performance of this play and are strongly cautioned to do so. If no such permission is obtained by the licensee, then the licensee must use only original materials and materials that the licensee owns and controls. Licensees are solely responsible and liable for clearances of all third-party copyrighted materials, and shall indemnify the copyright owners of the play(s) and their licensing agent, Concord Theatricals Corp., against any costs, expenses, losses and liabilities arising from the use of such copyrighted third-party materials by licensees. For music, please contact the appropriate music licensing authority in your territory for the rights to any incidental music not provided in connection with a performance license.

IMPORTANT BILLING AND CREDIT REQUIREMENTS

If you have obtained performance rights to this title, please refer to your licensing agreement for important billing and credit requirements.

SOMEWHERE OVER THE BORDER received Its world premiere on February 23, 2022, in a production by Syracuse Stage (Robert Hupp, Artistic Director; Jill Anderson, Managing Director), Syracuse, NY; and Geva Theatre Center (Mark Cuddy, Artistic Director; Christopher Mannelli, Executive Director), Rochester, NY; and Teatro Vista, Theatre with a View (Lorena Diaz and Wendy Mateo, Co-Artistic Directors), Chicago, IL.

The Syracuse Stage and Geva Theatre Center production was directed by Rebecca Martínez, with sets by Tanya Orellana, costumes by Asa Benally, lighting by Jennifer Fok, and sound by Jacqueline R. Herter. The dramaturg was Kristin Leahy. The music director was Julián Mesri. The production stage manager was Laura Jane Collins. The cast and band were as follows:

THE NARRATOR . . . . Arusi Santi
REINA . . . . Tanya De León
JULIA . . . . Francisca Muñoz
ADÁN, CRUZ . . . . Robert Ariza
NAPOLEON, SILVANO . . . . Bobby Plasencia
ANTONIA, LEONA . . . . Gloria Benavides
Keyboard, Band Leader. . . . . .Sarah Pool Wilhelm
Guitar. . . . . .Matt Pinto
Percussion . . . . Freddy Colon
Bass . . . . .Hector Diaz

The Teatro Vista production was directed by Denise Yvette Serna, with sets by Yvonne Miranda, costumes by Sarah Albrecht, lighting by Diane Fairchild, sound by Stefanie M. Senior, projections by Liviu Pasare, props by Lonnae Hickman, and puppets by Grace Needlman. The dramaturg was Kristin Leahy. The production stage manager was Madeline M. Scott. The cast and band were as follows:

THE NARRATOR . . . . Brian Quijada
REINA . . . . .Gabriela Moscoso
JULIA . . . . Claudia Quesada
ADÁN, CRUZ . . . . Tommy Rivera-Vega
NAPOLEON, SILVANO . . . . Andrés Enriquez
ANTONIA, LEONA . . . . Amanda Raquel Martinez
Covers. . . . . Ulyses Espinoza, Laura Quiñones, Jerreme Rodriguez,
Karla Serrato
Keyboard, Guitar . . . . .Yendrys Cespedes
Percussion . . . . Guido Acevedo
Bass . . . . .Roberto "Carpacho" Marin

SOMEWHERE OVER THE BORDER was written at the University of North Carolina at Greensboro, by invitation of Jim Wren.

CHARACTERS

THE NARRATOR – Our charming guide. Any age. Preferably plays guitar well.

REINA – A Salvadorean girl. 18 years old.

JULIA – Reina's mother. 40s.

ADÁN – Reina's brother. 20s.

NAPOLEON – A Salvadorean man who owns the restaurant that Reina works at.

ANTONIA – An older woman who lives in El Salvador and has a daughter in the United States.

CRUZ – An indigenous Guatemalan boy with dreams of obtaining an American degree.

SILVANO – A man from Tapachula, Mexico, with a dream to reunite with the rest of his family in America.

LEONA – A meek catholic nun from Guadalajara, with rock and roll dreams.

DOUBLING

ANTONIA and **LEONA** are played by the same actor.

DON NAPOLEON and **SILVANO** are played by the same actor.

ADÁN and **CRUZ** are played by the same actor.

THE NARRATOR also plays a **BUS DRIVER**, various **MEXICAN OFFICIALS**, Silvano's neighbor **RODRIGO**, **EL GRAN COYOTE DE TIJUANA**, and **FERNANDO**.

SETTING

Chanmico, Guatemala City, Tapachula, Guadalajara, Tijuana, and San Diego.

TIME

In the 1970s.

MUSICAL NUMBERS

01. Everyday Towns. . . . . The Narrator, Reina, Company
02. In the USA. . . . . . . Antonia, Reina, The Narrator, Company
02A. Scene Three Transition . . . . The Narrator
03. El Gran Coyote de Tijuana . . . . Napoleon, Reina, The Narrator, Company
03A. Gran Coyote Transition . . . . Instrumental
04. In the USA (Reprise) . . . . Reina, Adán
04A. Scene Five Transition. . . . . Instrumental
05. Somewhere Over the Border. . . . . Reina, The Narrator, Company
06. The Tornado . . . . . The Narrator, Antonia, Reina, Company
07. Beautiful Boy. . . . . Reina
07A. This Is It. . . . . Reina
08. Ride Up the Road (Guatemala) . . . . The Narrator, Reina
09. Cruz. . . . . Cruz, Reina
10. In the USA (Mini Reprise) . . . . Reina
11. Ride Up the Road (Tapachula). . . The Narrator, Reina, Cruz
12. What I Know. . . . . Julia
12A. Transition to Silvano's Inn. . . . . Instrumental
12B. In the USA (Final Reprise). . . . . Cruz
13. Silvano . . . . Silvano
13A. El Gran Coyote Reprise . . . . Reina, Silvano
14. Dream (Tapachula). . . . . The Narrator, Company
14A. Ride Up the Road (Guadalajara) . . . . . The Narrator, Reina, Cruz, Silvano
14B. Guadalajara Incidental . . . . Instrumental
15. Leona . . . . Leona
16. Dream (Guadalajara). The Narrator
17. Ride Up the Road (Tijuana) . . . . The Narrator, Reina, Cruz, Silvano, Leona
18. Red Skies . . . . Julia
18A. Coyote the Wizard . . . . Reina, Cruz, Silvano
18B. Kick in the Balls . . . . Instrumental
19. Desert (Part 1). . . . . Instrumental
20. Desert (Part 2). . . . . Reina, Cruz, Silvano, Leona
20A. Flower Truck . . . . Instrumental
21. Step by Step. . . . . Reina

Inspired by the real-life story of my mother, Reina Quijada, and L. Frank Baum's *The Wonderful Wizard of Oz*.

Scene One

Everyday Towns

(Lights up on **THE NARRATOR**. *He has a Cumbia-style band behind him. He begins to play the guitar strapped to him.)*

[MUSIC NO. 01 – EVERYDAY TOWNS]

THE NARRATOR. *Vaya Pues!*
THERE ARE TOWNS, LIKE MANY, MANY OTHER TOWNS
DIFF'RENT BUT SIMILAR TOWNS IN MANY OTHER
    COUNTRIES,

THE NARRATOR & COMPANY.
ALL ACROSS THE EARTH
WITH PEOPLE WHO GO 'BOUT THEIR DAYS
TRYING TO GIVE THEIR OWN LIFE SOME SORT OF WORTH

THE NARRATOR.
MAKIN' THE BEST OF THE BEST WITH WHAT THEY GOT
TOWNS WITH FORGOTTEN PEOPLE,
WHO LIVE WHETHER THEY HAVE THE MEANS OR NOT.

THE NARRATOR & COMPANY.
WORKING TO LIVE AND LIVING TO MAKE THEIR DREAMS
    COME TRUE
THE WORLD IS FILLED WITH DREAMERS, DREAMERS LIKE
    ME AND YOU.
DREAMERS LIKE ME AND YOU. DREAMERS LIKE ME AND
    YOU.

THE NARRATOR.
>EV'RYDAY DREAMERS. IN EV'RYDAY TOWNS.
>WITH COMMON EV'RYDAY PEOPLE
>OUT THERE MAKING THEIR ROUNDS.

THE NARRATOR & COMPANY.
>EV'RYDAY TOWNS WITH EV'RYDAY FOLK
>EV'RYDAY DREAMERS WITH STORIES THAT MUST BE TOLD.

Yo! *Que pasó? Qué'onda! Cómo estamos?* How you feeling? Welcome. *Bienvenidos.* There have been extraordinary everyday people since the beginning of man. Tonight, we rewind to 1978. We spin the globe and land on one place to look back at one everyday town like any other town called *Chanmico* in the country of *El Salvador*, lodged right up in there between *Honduras* and *Guatemala*. And in this everyday town we find an everyday girl like any other named Reina.

>(**REINA** *is lit. Her back is to the audience. She turns her head.*)

REINA. An everyday princess.

THE NARRATOR. Recently turned Seventeen.

And recently...pregnant.

>(*The* **COMPANY** *gasps.*)

But this is not a story about teen pregnancy!

I mean it is, but it isn't.

You see, Reina didn't know any better.

Dropped out of school at fourteen not out of disinterest,

but out of a necessity to work.

She was never told that *this (Re: her belly.)* might happen if another little thing happened to happen with a charming young boy, too young and naïve to stay.

She's the only girl in a family of brothers

All raised by Julia.

> (**JULIA** *is lit.*)

JULIA. A single mother.

THE NARRATOR. Now this is not a trait of all Salvadorean men. It just so happens that father figures don't really figure into this story.

Anyway! *Chanmico*, this everyday town, is their home!

> A TOWN, LIKE MANY, MANY OTHER TOWNS
> DIFF'RENT BUT SIMILAR TOWNS IN MANY OTHER
>   COUNTRIES,

THE NARRATOR & COMPANY.
> ALL ACROSS THE EARTH
> WITH PEOPLE WHO GO 'BOUT THEIR DAYS
> TRYIN' TO GIVE THEIR OWN LIFE SOME SORT OF WORTH

And like any common everyday story, this story begins with the most worthy of worthy reasons. This story begins with life.

> (**REINA** *births her baby.* **JULIA** *is there.*)

COMPANY EXCEPT REINA.
> AHH. AHH. AHH. AHH.

> (**REINA** *birthing the baby.*)

Ahhhh!

> (**REINA** *wraps her baby up in a blanket.*)

THE NARRATOR. Little Baby Fernando! Now, most of us can agree that babies are adorable, and they change you forever and add so much happiness to your life, but they can also RUIN IT! You will not sleep and you will rely on coffee 'til the end of days! *(To audience member.)* You know what I'm talking about!

THE NARRATOR.   On top of that, the situation in this everyday town of *Chanmico* is, well...

> LET ME PAINT THE PICTURE, LET ME BE SUPER CLEAR
> LET ME PAINT THE PICTURE, LET ME BE SUPER CLEAR.

Things are not okay here.

Nah, cuz as all of you damn well know, every place can get dark and grey sometimes. Every place can experience civil unrest. Nationwide division. Protests against the government. It is 1978 y'all and a Civil War is on the horizon in *El Salvador*.

And we're not stopping there! *Nombre!*

Even if there wasn't a war coming, consider the endless hours of work to barely make ends meet, now add an extra mouth to feed.

Puchica!

> THE GRIND IS A SERIOUS THING.
> PROVE YOURSELF BY WORK ETHIC AND THE COIN YOU
>   CAN BRING IN
> YOU WORK SO YOU DON'T ROB OR STEAL
> HONEST, THE GRIND IS REAL.

THE NARRATOR & COMPANY.

> YOU WORK AND WORK AND WORK AND WORK AND WORK
> AND SERVE AND SERVE AND SERVE TO GET WHAT YOU
>   DESERVE

THE NARRATOR.

> AND IN THIS EV'RYDAY TOWN, THE PAYOFF IS LESS THAN
>   EV'RYDAY
> AND IF YOU PRESS THEM AND SAY,
> "HEY, I NEED MORE PAY!"
> THEY MIGHT SAY "OKAY, GOODBYE, WE'LL GRAB THE
>   NEXT PERSON IN LINE. THAT'S FINE, THEY'VE BEEN
>   WAITING."
> PENNILESS AND UNEMPLOYED, YOUR FUTURE STARTS
>   FADING

THE NARRATOR & COMPANY.
> THE GRIND IS A SERIOUS THING.
> PROVE YOURSELF BY WORK ETHIC AND THE COIN YOU
>   CAN BRING IN.

THE NARRATOR.
> AND REINA IS PART OF THIS SYSTEM, THIS EXPECTED
>   WORK HORSE EXTREME
> SHE COOKS AND CLEANS AT HOME AND GOES TO TOWN
>   TO WAITRESS AND SELL THE FARM'S COFFEE BEANS
> REINA GETS UP EV'RY MORNING WHEN THE BABY CRIES,
>   BEFORE THE ROOSTER CROWS.
> AND SHE PUSHES THROUGH HER JOBS WHILE A CLOCK
>   NEVER STOPS, A LIFE OF FEW HIGHS IN A WORLD OF
>   MANY LOWS.

THE NARRATOR & REINA.	**COMPANY.**
EV'RYDAY. DAY IN, DAY OUT.	EV'RYDAY.
DROWNING IN	DAY IN, DAY OUT.
RESPONSIBILITIES.	
THREE MEALS A DAY IS RARE	
AND A FULL NIGHT'S SLEEP,	FULL NIGHT'S SLEEP
IS NOTHING BUT A DREAM.	DREAM, DREAM, DREAM!

JULIA. You're off to a late / start.

REINA. Well Fernando kept waking up / in the middle of the night.

JULIA. That's no excuse. There's work / to be done.

REINA. I know. I have to head down to the lagoon / to do laundry.

JULIA. Your brothers are already out on the field, so / do that quickly.

REINA. Yes mother.

JULIA. You'll also have to help work the Porteros' field this morning.

REINA. They can't work their own field?

JULIA. They're gone.

REINA. Gone? Where?

JULIA. God knows. They took all their things. The National
Guard shootings in San Salvador must've scared them.
(Scoffs.)

THE NARRATOR & COMPANY.
EV'RYDAY. DAY IN, DAY OUT.

JULIA. *Pasmádos.*

So, we're gonna take over their farm. Bunch of ungrateful
idiotas. So hurry up. Get your work done here before
you head out to the market.

THE NARRATOR & COMPANY.
DREAM. DREAM. DREAM

> (**REINA** *heads down the hill to the Chanmico
> Lagoon where she washes and cleans their
> laundry, trying to scrub away an endless
> dust from their clothes.)*

REINA.

YOU WORK AND WORK AND WORK	
AND WORK AND WORK	
AND SERVE AND SERVE AND SERVE	
TO GET WHAT YOU DESERVE.	**COMPANY**.
PEOPLE WORK, PEOPLE STAY, PEOPLE	AH
RUN AWAY.	AH
WILL THIS LIFE THAT WE LIVE,	AH
ALWAYS STAY THIS WAY.	AH
WILL WE EVER BREATHE?	AH
WHEN SO MANY LEAVE,	AH
I WONDER IF THEY ALL SEE	AH
SOMETHING WE DON'T	

AND IF SO, MY MOTHER WOULDN'T
 ADMIT IT
BUT IT'S OBVIOUS THE COUNTRY HAS
 SHIFTED
SO GREY.
AND I DON'T WANT MY SON TO DIE

	AH
AND WHAT IF ALL MY WORK RUNS DRY	AH AH
I HAVE NO OTHER OPTIONS TO TRY.	AH AH
WE'RE BARELY GETTING BY,	AH
AND I WISH WE COULD JUST FLY	AH AH
	FLY

AWAY.

JULIA. *(From offstage.)* Reina!!

  (**REINA** *grabs her clothes in one hand,*
  Fernando in the other, and runs off.)

THE NARRATOR.
 WORKING TO LIVE OR LIVING TO MAKE THEIR DREAMS
  COME TRUE
 THE WORLD IS FILLED WITH DREAMERS, DREAMERS LIKE
  ME AND YOU.
 DREAMERS LIKE ME AND YOU, DREAMERS LIKE ME AND
  YOU.

THE NARRATOR & COMPANY.
 EV'RYDAY TOWNS, WITH EV'RYDAY FOLK
 EV'RYDAY PEOPLE WITH STORIES THAT MUST BE TOLD.

  (Transition.)

Scene Two

Village Market

(A small coffee bean stand is lit. **REINA** *stands behind it.* **ANTONIA** *enters unseen.)*

ANTONIA. Say cheese!

> *(***ANTONIA*** *snaps a picture of* ***REINA*** *and baby Fernando with a Polaroid Instant Camera.)*

REINA. Whoa!

ANTONIA. Oh that was a good one!

REINA. What is that?

ANTONIA. It's my new camera! It prints out a color photograph! *Mira Mira!*

> *(***ANTONIA*** *hands* ***REINA*** *the Polaroid picture.)*

Here.

REINA. There's nothing here.

ANTONIA. Give it a little shake shake.

> *(***REINA*** *does a little shimmy with it.)*

Put your hips into it! Trust me I'm the expert on the shake shakes, it's how I tricked my Ernesto into marriage.

REINA. *(Re: Polaroid.)* I guess I have a lot to learn. Still blank.

ANTONIA. It takes a bit. Don't worry. You'll get there.

REINA. So, where have you been all summer? I was worried something had happened to you.

ANTONIA. Oh I know. I heard about the massacre at the University. *Qué desmadre.* How's your family though? Everybody safe?

REINA. We're okay. For now. But people are leaving. Our neighbors The Porteros have already taken off.

ANTONIA. Oh yes, I heard they lost their son in the shootings. *(Beat.) Ay* Reina, I used to live and breathe *chisme* but now the only thing *chisme* gives me is hot flashes!

REINA. Oh. So, where were you?

ANTONIA. Oh, I spent the summer in The United States with my daughter Soyla in her beautiful home in California. Helping to take care of *her* newborn baby.

REINA. Doña! You're a grandma?

ANTONIA. *(Flips her hair.)* I know!

REINA. Wow!

ANTONIA. Babies, babies, babies.

She has two now. The older one's five.

Look!

> *(**ANTONIA** takes out some Polaroid pictures and shows them to **REINA**.)*

That's my daughter right there. And there are my grandkids. Aren't they beautiful?

REINA. *(Eyes still glued on the picture.)* That's a lovely home she has.

ANTONIA. It's her apartment. She split from the children's father and moved into her own place. It's for the better. Trust me. Boy was a *bochinchero.*

REINA. She lives there alone? How long has she been in the States?

ANTONIA. She was about your age when she left.

REINA. Really?

ANTONIA. Yup. She's a citizen there now. And last year she had my papers squared away so I could come visit. I flew there and back.

REINA. You got on a plane?

ANTONIA. Sure did.

REINA. Weren't you scared?

ANTONIA. No! It was luxurious! I forgot I was sitting in a chair in the sky! I had a beautiful blonde *gringa* lady bringing me things, a half-chicken right to my seat, peanuts, and she even helped me light my cigarette. I don't even smoke, but everyone else was smoking so I said, "screw it! I'm living large!"

REINA. Wow. And your daughter, she's raising the kids all on her own?

[MUSIC NO. 02 – IN THE USA]

ANTONIA. Yes! And she hasn't gone crazy like I did. It's a miracle! Oh God...

California. Reina! America, it's something else.

HOW BEAUTIFUL THAT LIFE IS!

IN THE USA, IT SEEMS LIKE LIFE IS ENDLESS

THE YOUNG KIDS ARE STRESS FREE AND THE OLD FOLKS ARE RICH

OLD PEOPLE, YOUNG PEOPLE, SICK PEOPLE, HEALTHY PEOPLE I CAN'T EVEN TELL YOU WHICH IS WHICH

THE SCHOOLS ARE BETTER WHICH MEANS THE KIDS ARE HAPPY.

AN UPBRINGING SO DIFF'RENT THAN THAT OF THEIR GRANNIES.

ANTONIA.

THE STREETS, THE TREES,
THE SUNLIGHT, COLORS
I'VE NEVER SEEN
THE WATER, RESTAURANTS,
AND BATHROOMS
ARE SO FREAKING CLEAN!

THE NARRATOR & REINA.

THE STREETS, THE TREES,
THE SUNLIGHT,

THE NARRATOR & COMPANY.

HOW BEAUTIFUL THAT
LIFE IS!
IN THE USA, IT SEEMS
LIKE LIFE IS ENDLESS
IN THE USA. IN THE USA
EV'RYONE IS OUT, TAKING
IN THE SUN
BURNT SKIN IS NOT A
MARK OF WORK, IT'S
DESIRED BY EV'RYONE
TIME IS A PLENTY
TIME FOR YOURSELF, AND
TIME FOR THE KIDS,
AND THE INCOME IS
STEADY
WHICH MEANS YOU AREN'T
PINCHING PENNIES
AND YOU DON'T HAVE
BELLIES GROAN
AND YOU CAN WORK ONE
JOB AND BE FINE AND
BUILD A HOME OF
YOUR VERY OWN.
HOW BEAUTIFUL THAT
LIFE IS!
IN THE USA, IT SEEMS
LIKE LIFE IS ENDLESS
IN THE USA, YOU CAN JUST
FEEL IT IN THE AIR

HOW BEAUTIFUL THAT
LIFE IS!
USA

USA

AH

CHA LA LA LA

THE NARRATOR & COMPANY.

HOW BEAUTIFUL THAT
LIFE IS!
USA,

USA

REINA.

> OUT THERE, IT FEELS LIKE LIFE IS A BIT MORE FAIR.
> IN THE USA, IN THE USA
>
> A HOME, OF YOUR OWN, AND THREE MEALS A DAY
> SOMETHING SO FAR-FETCHED HERE, IS THE AMERICAN
>   WAY

It almost doesn't sound real. So why don't you just stay out there?

ANTONIA. Ernesto's mother is sick and we need to be here for her final days.

REINA. Ay. Doña. I'm so sorry.

ANTONIA. No, it's okay. I hate my mother-in-law. And good news, when she dies, we're getting her farm. Yay!

REINA. Oh. Yay.

ANTONIA. Okay check your picture now.

> *(They both look at the picture.* **REINA***'s heart melts.)*

That Fernando is a little piece of *semita dulce*, isn't he?

REINA. Thanks Doña. I hope one day I can give him all the things your grandkids have.

ANTONIA. Oh, I know you will. So…?

REINA. So what?

ANTONIA. Unless you expect me to die right here, I need my beans sweetie! Let's bag it up!

> *(They laugh.)*

> *(Lights transition as* **REINA** *contemplates.)*

Scene Three

Napoleon's Pupuseria

THE NARRATOR. Ugh, the USA sounds so good I know! But no time to daydream though! On to the next job at Napoleon's *Pupuseria*!

[MUSIC NO. 02A – SCENE THREE TRANSITION]

YOU WORK AND WORK AND WORK AND WORK.
AND SERVE AND SERVE AND SERVE.

And after a long night...

> (**REINA** *is finishing cleaning the restaurant. Fernando is in a basket on a table.* **NAPOLEON** *hands her her pay.*)

NAPOLEON. Here ya go Reinita.

REINA. Thank you.

> (**REINA** *sits and looks at her money, disappointedly.*)

NAPOLEON. I know. It's been so slow. The protests have been really messing with our sales.

REINA. *(She sighs.)* Lord. Will it ever be enough?

NAPOLEON. Listen, you've worked so hard for me since you were a *bichita* and you deserve so much more. We'll get through this.

> (**REINA** *is silent. Then...*)

REINA. Don Napo, have you heard of The USA?

NAPOLEON. *(Beat.)* Have I heard of the enormous country above *Mexico*?

No, never. Tell me.

REINA. Well, it's a place / where you can –

NAPOLEON. I know what it is. *No soy baboso.* Why do you ask?

REINA. No, it's just...

I talked to a lady at the Village Market today and she told me about her daughter in The United States.

NAPOLEON. Antonia? The shakey shakes lady?

REINA. Yes!

NAPOLEON. Ah yes. I helped her daughter Soyla cross many years ago.

REINA. You did?!

NAPOLEON. Yes – wait. You aren't thinking about taking this little guy with you, are you?

REINA. I don't know.

NAPOLEON. It's very dangerous. And expensive.

REINA. Why?

NAPOLEON. It's illegal.

REINA. Is there a legal way?

NAPOLEON. You can apply. But Don Lipo from Santa Ana died waiting for them to respond. And you can go to seek asylum but they'll usually just make you turn around. You remember Tito, who used to work in the kitchen? He got involved with some *gangeros*, left to seek asylum, was denied, and was forced to come back. A week later...well...we all sent his mother flowers.

REINA. So, tell me the illegal way.

NAPOLEON. Reina, I just want you to keep in mind that the journey is tough and –

REINA. I get it, it's dangerous and people die. People are also dying in the streets here. From gunfire or from starvation. You pick. Please. I'm just curious.

[MUSIC NO. 03 – EL GRAN COYOTE DE TIJUANA]

NAPOLEON. Okay. *(Beat.)* There's a man you need to see.
He goes by...

EL GRAN COYOTE DE TIJUANA.
HE'S THE ONE THAT YOU NEED WHEN YOU WANNA ... GO.
WHEN YOU'VE PACKED A BAG AND LEAVE CHANMICO.
HE'S THE ONE AT THE END OF THE ROAD.
HE'S THE ONE THAT HAS GRACIOUSLY SHOWED
PLENTY OF FRIENDS OF MINE TO THEIR NEW HOME
SPENDS HIS TIME HELPING FOLKS THROUGH THE
    UNKNOWN.
IF YOU'RE IN SEARCH OF A LIFE SOMEWHERE OVER THE
    BORDER
YOU ORDER A DREAM, AND HE'LL DELIVER THE WAY
AS LONG AS YOU HAVE ONE THOUSAND FIVE HUNDRED
    PESOS TO PAY.

ADÁN, JULIA & ANTONIA. *(From offstage.)* Whoo!

REINA. One thousand five hundred?

NAPOLEON.
THAT'S RIGHT. IT'S NOT CHEAP.
BUT HE PROMISES THE AMERICAN DREAM TO KEEP.
IF YOU CAN KEEP UP, YOU CAN CLEAN UP.
MAKE YOUR AMERICAN DREAMS COME TRUE
THAT'S WHAT EL COYOTE DE TIJUANA CAN DO FOR YOU.

NAPOLEON, THE NARRATOR, ANTONIA & ADÁN.
EL GRAN COYOTE DE TIJUANA

NAPOLEON.
HE'S THE ONE THAT YOU NEED WHEN YOU GOTTA ... GO.
HE'S THE ONE WHO KNOWS HOW TO AVOID THE BORDER
    PATROL
AND STROLL INTO THE LAND THAT YOU DREAM ABOUT
HERE IN THE SOUTH, HE'S THE WIZARD OF METHOD

NAPOLEON.
> TRIED AND TESTED, I CAN TELL YOU WHERE YOU'RE
> HEADED
> JUST FOLLOW THE ROAD ON THE BUS AND KEEP QUIET

NAPOLEON, THE NARRATOR, ANTONIA & ADÁN.
> IF YOU HAVE A NEED TO GO,

NAPOLEON.
> REINA, I KNOW, YOU CANNOT DENY IT

NAPOLEON, THE NARRATOR, ANTONIA & ADÁN.
> EL GRAN COYOTE DE TIJUANA

NAPOLEON.
> HE'S THE ONE THAT YOU NEED WHEN YOU WANNA ...
> GO.

REINA.
> I SEE. I SEE.
> THAT'S THE MAN I'D NEED.

COMPANY.
> EL GRAN COYOTE DE TIJUANA
> HE'S THE ONE THAT YOU NEED WHEN YOU WANNA ...

NAPOLEON.
> GO.

[MUSIC NO. 03A – GRAN COYOTE TRANSITION]

NAPOLEON. One thousand five hundred Mexican pesos to the wizard. That's what it's gonna take to get you to the majestic Green everyone talks about.

REINA. Majestic Green?

NAPOLEON. Yeah.

> Your Green Card.

REINA. A Green Card?

NAPOLEON. Yes. It allows you to work.

REINA. Ah, I see. Got it.

NAPOLEON. And some people make it so far, they prosper and send money back. Like Soyla does for Antonia.

REINA. My mother would wring my neck if I left.

NAPOLEON. *Sí, vea.* Julia would rip my tongue out if she found out I helped you.

But look, I pulled out of the family sugar cane business to start this restaurant. My mother didn't talk to me for months. But when she ate my *pupusas*, a recipe she taught me, do you think she still held a grudge?

REINA. No.

NAPOLEON. Of course, she did! She's a Salvadorean woman. BUT! She was proud that people from all over were coming to taste her recipe. But most importantly, I did what made me happy.

REINA. Thanks Don Napo.

(Transition.)

Scene Four

Brotherly Love

THE NARRATOR. Who knew Don Napo had so much flow?!

After work Adán, her brother, picks up Reina and Fernando to walk home.

(**ADÁN** *waits for* **REINA**.)

ADÁN. Hey sis!

How'd you do at the market this morning?

Cuz I did horrible! I sold no milk. Which is terrible because Chula is pumping out that milk like it's soft serve! I'm having to drink it myself to make sure Mom doesn't notice! How 'bout you?

REINA. I saw Doña Toña at the market today.

ADÁN. Oh yeah? That lady with the shakey shakes? That witch is rich! She get you good?

[MUSIC NO. 04 – IN THE USA (REPRISE)]

REINA.
SHE JUST GOT BACK FROM CALIFORNIA
HER DAUGHTER LIVES THERE WITH TWO KIDS OF HER OWN
SHE SHOWED ME SOME PICTURES
OF THESE TWO PRETTY GIRLS, AMERICAN-GROWN.
IN A ONE-PARENT HOME.
HOW SWEET.
HOW BEAUTIFUL THAT LIFE SOUNDS
IN THE USA,

ADÁN.
WITH A BUNCH OF GRINGOS ALL AROUND

REINA.
BUT IN THE USA, THE SCHOOLS ARE SO MUCH BETTER

ADÁN.
AND IN THE USA, THEY HAVE CRAPPIER WEATHER

REINA.
IN THE USA, I COULD AFFORD BABY FOOD FOR HIM TO EAT.

ADÁN.
BUT IN EL SALVADOR, YOUR BREAST MILK IS ALWAYS FREE.

REINA. Shoes, Adán.
THEY WERE WEARING SHOES.
SUCH A SMALL LITTLE THING
BUT IF I HAD A LIFE TO CHOOSE,
I'D CHOOSE THE ONE WHERE MY SON OWNED SHOES
    BEFORE THE AGE OF TEN
CUZ EVEN GRINDING AWAY EV'RY DAY HERE I WON'T DO
    THAT BY THEN.

ADÁN.
SO, HE'LL WEAR THONGS LIKE HIS UNCLE A, THEY WORK
    FOR ME
EASY TO SLIP ON AND THEY LET THE TOES BREATHE.

REINA. Stop with the jokes.

ADÁN. We'll be *chancla* buddies!

REINA. I'm serious.

ADÁN. I know you want the best life for the little guy. I do too!

REINA.
YOU UNDERSTAND ME THEN, DON'T YOU NOW OLDER
    BROTHER?
I COULD RAISE YOUR NEPHEW PROPER EVEN AS A SINGLE
    MOTHER.

REINA & ADÁN.
HOW BEAUTIFUL THAT LIFE SOUNDS
IN THE USA,

REINA.
> IT JUST DOESN'T SEEM QUITE AS BAD
> IN THE USA, HE COULD LIVE HAPPY WITHOUT A DAD

ADÁN. She's really doing it alone out there? Huh?

REINA. Yes, and thriving.

REINA & ADÁN.
> IN THE USA,

REINA.
> HE'D HAVE A BETTER LIFE

REINA & ADÁN.
> A BETTER LIFE, THAN WE HAVE.

ADÁN. Welp, too bad the USA is like a million kilometers away. What a shame.

> (**ADÁN** *starts to go.*)

REINA. Adán?

Don Napo says he knows a person who could help me get to the States.

ADÁN. What?

REINA. For one thousand five hundred Mexican pesos.

ADÁN. We don't have that much money! And what about Fernando?

REINA. I could probably take him...

> (**ADÁN** *shoots* **REINA** *a look.*)

No, I can't take him. Don Napo says it's too dangerous. *(Frustrated sigh.)*

ADÁN. ...

You're serious?

> (**REINA** *nods.*)

Wow.

> *(Beat.)*

REINA. I'll go, pick up a Green Card and come back for Fernando as fast as I can. He won't even notice. And then I could put in for your papers too. And eventually fly you and Mom and the guys out like Soyla does for Antonia. And I can send Mom money. Or we can all go.

ADÁN. So, Mom chops us all up into pieces and makes *pupusas* out of us? No thanks, I think I'll stay here.

> **(REINA** *smiles sadly.)*

But hey, maybe that sounds fun for you. What do I know, sis? Come on.

[MUSIC NO. 04A – SCENE FIVE TRANSITION]

Scene Five

Somewhere Over the Border

THE NARRATOR. When Reina gets home that evening,

> (**ADÁN** *gives* **JULIA** *some money and exits.*)

JULIA. So?

REINA. Hello / mother.

JULIA. What did you bring home?

REINA. I picked up some rice at the market / for us.

JULIA. And?

REINA. I also picked up some soap. I used the last of it / on the laundry.

JULIA. And? Come on Reina.

I need to pay the meat and cheese lady tomorrow. It's been two weeks.

REINA. Okay.

> (**REINA** *reaches into her bag and hands her money.*)

JULIA. That's it?

REINA. I have a little more but –

JULIA. We're short. We'll need all the money you made today. Provisions for the house / are what's important.

REINA. What about the boys? Have they not brought any in?

JULIA. Adán contributed. And *we've* been out in the field all day.

> (**REINA** *sighs. She hands* **JULIA** *all the money.*)

JULIA. Don't take that tone with me.

>   *(Baby Fernando starts to cry.)*

Good God control that child! / Have you fed him?

REINA. He's teething mother.

Yes!

JULIA. Shhh. Quiet down, my pretty. He just needs to fall
asleep –

>   *(**JULIA** goes to the basket to pick up Fernando.
>   **JULIA** jolts back.)*

Ahh!

REINA. What?

JULIA. He bit me!

>   *(Fernando cries more.)*

REINA. I told you / he was teething

JULIA. Take him outside. And while you're out there bring
the laundry in. It should be dry by now.

REINA. Yes mother.

[MUSIC NO. 05 – SOMEWHERE OVER THE BORDER]

THE NARRATOR.
>   YOU WORK AND WORK AND WORK AND WORK AND WORK
>   AND SERVE AND SERVE AND SERVE – Jesus! Even singing
>   it is exhausting!!

>   *(**REINA** has a basket for clothes and a basket
>   with Fernando in it. She unclips clothes off the
>   clothesline and folds as she sings to her baby.)*

REINA.
> I GUESS I SHOULDN'T COMPLAIN.
> I SHOULD JUST STAY IN MY LANE
> CUZ WE'VE GOT CLOTHES ON OUR BACKS AND A ROOF
>   OVER OUR HEADS
> AND I DO MY VERY BEST TO KEEP US FED.
>
> BUT I KNOW FOR A GIRL MY AGE
> WITH A BABY AND NO LIVABLE WAGE
> THAT SOMETHING'S GOTTA CHANGE.
> CUZ WE CAN'T LIVE THIS WAY.
>
> AND I FEEL THIS PLACE ISN'T MY HOME
> BUT I KNOW MY MOM WOULD FREAK, IF I SAID I'D WANT
>   TO GO
> BUT I'D DO IT EVEN SO
> CUZ YOUR GRANDMA, SHE TRULY BELIEVES
> THAT WE SHOULD BE GRATEFUL AND WE SHOULDN'T
>   LEAVE.
> BUT I DISAGREE,
> AND WHAT HAS WORKED FOR HER, HAS NOT WORKED
>   FOR ME
>
> WE DON'T SEE EYE TO EYE, I KNOW THAT YOU DESERVE
>   MUCH MORE
> A LIFE WITH NO HARDSHIP
> AND NO FEAR OF LOOMING WAR
> I KNOW OF THE LIFE, THAT'S PERFECT I SWEAR
> WHERE WE COULD BE RICH AND BE VERY SAFE OUT THERE
>
> SOMEWHERE OVER THE BORDER
> SOMEWHERE WE CAN BREATHE FREE
> SOMEWHERE OVER THE BORDER
> JUST YOU AND ME
>
> AND WE WON'T BOTHER
> TO TELL YOUR GRANDMOTHER
> CUZ SHE MIGHT URGE ME STAY
> AND IF SHE DOES, I WON'T WANT TO DISOBEY

BUT SOMETHINGS GOTTA CHANGE.
CUZ WE CAN'T LIVE THIS WAY.

AND I DON'T EVEN KNOW WHERE I'D GO
BUT I KNOW I MUST GO ALONE
IT'S TOO DANGEROUS FOR US BOTH

AND THOUGH WE'LL TEMPORARILY BE PARTED
I KNOW THAT'LL BE THE HARDEST PART
HOME IS ONLY WHERE THE HEART IS
AND THAT'S WHEREVER YOU ARE

COMPANY EXCEPT JULIA.
SOMEWHERE OVER THE BORDER

REINA.
THAT'S WHERE OUR HOME WILL BE

COMPANY EXCEPT JULIA.
SOMEWHERE OVER THE BORDER

REINA.

JUST YOU AND ME	**COMPANY EXCEPT JULIA.**
CUZ I	I
WANT THAT PERFECT LIFE.	

(Lights fade as she collects her folded laundry and goes inside the house.)

Scene Six

The Tornado

THE NARRATOR. Reina is ready to go! So, every day that week, Reina works her ass off. Slinging *pupusas* at the restaurant, selling coffee and helping her brothers out on the farm. Doing every little bit extra she can to save up.

[MUSIC NO. 06 – THE TORNADO]

YOU WORK AND WORK AND WORK AND WORK AND WORK
AND SERVE AND SERVE AND SERVE TO GET WHAT YOU
    DESERVE

But the following weekend, Saturday, would turn out to be a storm of events.

> *(Music plays like a whirlwind.)*

THE TORNADO ROARS
AND WHEN IT RAINS IT POURS
IT'S THE STORM THAT MAKES YOU WALK OUT THE DOOR
HAPPENS SO QUICK, HAPPENS SO FAST
OOH! LIFE CAN TAKE OFF IN A BLAST
THE TORNADO ROARS
AND WHEN IT RAINS IT POURS
IT'S THE STORM THAT MAKES YOU WALK OUT THE DOOR
LEAVING THE OLD A QUICK MEM'RY OF THE PAST
NO MOMENT TO THINK ABOUT WHICH MEM'RIES WILL
    LAST

> *(Transition to the weekend farmer's market. Music underscores.)*

> *(**REINA** is at her coffee stand. **ANTONIA** enters.)*

ANTONIA. You have a bag of beans for me?

REINA. Of course. Here ya go!

ANTONIA. Mmm. Thank you dear.

REINA. Hey!

So, I've been thinking a lot.

About what you told me last week.

ANTONIA. Oh lord. What did I say? Was I drinking?

REINA. No! California.

ANTONIA. Oh yes!

REINA. I'm going.

ANTONIA. Really?

REINA. Yes! I'm saving up!

ANTONIA. Reina. Listen.

There's nothing that would make me happier than to help you.

REINA. What do you mean?

ANTONIA. You always brighten my day and your ambition reminds me so much of my Soyla. How does borrowing 800 *colones* sound? And you can pay my daughter back once you get to The USA?

REINA. That's like half of what I need!

ANTONIA. I'll talk to Soyla about it today. She could pick you up once you get to the States and help you from there! I'll drop off the money at your house later on.

REINA. No!

ANTONIA. No?

REINA. No! My mother doesn't know I'm going. And if she found out, she'd –

ANTONIA. She'd bury you alive, yeah. Understood. I'll drop the money off with your brother Adán.

(**ANTONIA** *smiles.* **REINA** *hugs her.*)

THE NARRATOR & ANTONIA.
THE TORNADO ROARS
AND WHEN IT RAINS IT POURS
IT'S THE STORM THAT MAKES YOU WALK OUT THE DOOR

THE NARRATOR.
HAPPENS SO QUICK,   **ANTONIA.**
                           HAPPENS SO QUICK,
HAPPENS SO FAST   HAPPENS SO FAST
OOH! LIFE CAN TAKE OFF   AH
    IN A BLAST.

(*Pulsing music continues to underscore, getting faster and more intense.*)

NAPOLEON. What a night! Great work!

(**NAPOLEON** *counts the moneybox.*)

REINA. Yeah? Well, I'm really stepping it up now!

NAPOLEON. Oh yeah? Why's that?

REINA. I'm saving up for *El Gran Coyote de Tijuana*!

NAPOLEON. Wow! Well, had I known you were trying to leave immediately I would have given to you sooner!

REINA. What do you mean Don Napo?

(**NAPOLEON** *reaches into the moneybox and whips out a wad of cash.*)

NAPOLEON. Here.

THE NARRATOR & ANTONIA.
AH AH

REINA. Don Napo.

NAPOLEON. And don't worry about paying me back.

REINA. Don Napo!

> (**REINA** *hugs* **NAPOLEON**. **ADÁN** *enters.*)

ADÁN. Hey! What are we celebrating?!

> (**ADÁN** *joins in on the hug.*)

REINA. Adán! Don Napo just gave me money to help me!

ADÁN. Don Napo?

You're the man!

NAPOLEON. Aww come on! I'm just a guy. I mean, I have a huge heart and I'm still single, so tell all your friends, but I never had kids of my own, so I want to help you.

ADÁN. Well about that... Reina?

Here.

> (**ADÁN** *hands her a wad of cash.*)

THE NARRATOR & ANTONIA.

AH AH

REINA. What is this?

ADÁN. Count it!

> (**REINA** *does.*)

REINA. How did you get this??

ADÁN. I sold Chula.

REINA. Adán!

ADÁN. I know how much this means to you. And you mean more to me than a cow.

Also, I was getting pretty tired of drinking her milk? So now do you have enough?

REINA. Yes!

NAPOLEON. You could even leave tomorrow! The bus to *Guatemala* is every day at five a.m.

ADÁN. Just like that!

NAPOLEON. I'll tell Antonia and we can all walk you to the bus!

REINA. I need to pack!

THE NARRATOR & COMPANY.
THE TORNADO ROARS
AND WHEN IT RAINS IT POURS
IT'S THE STORM THAT MAKES YOU WALK OUT THE DOOR

THE TORNADO ROARS
AND WHEN IT RAINS IT POURS
IT'S THE STORM THAT MAKES YOU WALK OUT THE DOOR

THE NARRATOR.
HAPPENS SO QUICK,   **COMPANY.**
                                                              HAPPENS SO QUICK

THE NARRATOR & COMPANY.
HAPPENS SO FAST

THE NARRATOR, REINA & JULIA.
OOH! LIFE CAN TAKE OFF IN A BLAST

THE NARRATOR & REINA.   **COMPANY.**
LEAVING THE OLD A   AH
    QUICK MEM'RY OF THE
    PAST
NO MOMENT TO THINK   AH
    ABOUT WHICH
    MEM'RIES WILL LAST
NO MOMENT TO THINK
    ABOUT
                                                        THINK ABOUT
WHICH MEM'RIES WILL
    LAST

Scene Seven

Goodbyes

(It's the middle of the night.)

*(In a few hours she'll be leaving for the bus. Everything that **REINA** has been working for has happened and the only thing left to do is say goodbye.)*

*(The lights shift to **REINA** and Fernando's crib.)*

[MUSIC NO. 07 – BEAUTIFUL BOY]

REINA.
LET ME HAVE A LOOK,
AT MY BEAUTIFUL BOY.
I'M GONNA MISS YOUR LITTLE FACE
I'LL COUNT THE DAYS
'TIL I SEE YOU AND HUG YOU AGAIN.
YOU AND I
WE'LL REUNITE
WE'RE GONNA MAKE IT THROUGH THE DARKNESS,
    THROUGH THE NIGHT
I HAVE TO GO
THE USA WAITS FOR ME
AND THOUGH I'M SCARED TO MY BONES
AND I DON'T KNOW WHAT LIES AHEAD
I HAVE TO FIND US ANOTHER HOME.
WHERE YOU AND I
WON'T HAVE TO STRUGGLE
IT'LL ALL BE WORTH THE TROUBLE AND PAIN
THIS IS GOODBYE
BUT I WILL RETURN FOR YOU
'TIL THEN I HOPE YOU DON'T CRY

REINA.

    I'M GONNA TRY WITH ALL MY MIGHT TO MAKE THIS ALL
        AS FAST AS A DREAM.
    THEN YOU AND I
    WE'LL BE TOGETHER
    IN ANOTHER PLACE THAT'S BETTER FOR US
    'TIL THEN JUST SLEEP
    MY BEAUTIFUL BOY.

        (**REINA** *leaves a letter in the crib.* **REINA** *grabs
        her bag and quietly walks out of her house.*)

THE NARRATOR. And waiting outside...

[MUSIC NO. 07A – THIS IS IT]

NAPOLEON. Reina. Here. As promised.

ADÁN. Ready?

ANTONIA. You have everything you need?

REINA. Yup.

NAPOLEON. Good. So, remember, do not mention anything
about *El Gran Coyote*. Do not mention my name to
anyone. Do not say anything about going to the USA.
Say you are just taking a trip to Mexico City. That's it.

REINA. Got it.

NAPOLEON. You are going to get on four buses. One from
here to *Guatemala*. One from *Guatemala* to *Tapachula,
Mexico. Tapachula* to *Guadalajara*. And finally,
Guadalajara to *Tijuana* to meet *El Gran Coyote*. You'll
recognize him from his booming voice. You'll only have to
spend the night in *Tapachula* and *Guadalajara*. Got it?

REINA. Got it.

        (**REINA** *seems overwhelmed.* **ADÁN** *notices.*)

ADÁN. You'll be fine. Fernando will be fine. I'll take care
of him.

REINA. Okay.

ANTONIA. And if you can, have a little *gringo* boy fall in love with you and have him marry you. Trust me honey it'll save you a heap load of trouble. *(Winks.)*

REINA. Um...okay. I'll try.

THE NARRATOR. When they get to the bus station it finally dawns.

REINA.
THIS IS IT.

NAPOLEON. It sure is.

REINA.
THE TIME IS UP.

ANTONIA. Time to go.

REINA.
I'M GETTING ON THIS BUS.

NAPOLEON. Remember to keep your hopes high and your head down low.

REINA.
THIS IS THE ROAD THAT I'LL BE RIDING.

NAPOLEON. Yes.

REINA.
WHY DO I FEEL LIKE CRYING?

ANTONIA. It's okay. It's gonna be okay.

REINA. Don Napo, Adán, Doña Toña?

NAPOLEON, ADÁN & ANTONIA. Yes?

REINA. Thank you.

ADÁN. Go ahead sis. Now on your way.

THE NARRATOR. And with a blown kiss goodbye, Reina boards the bus bound for the USA.

Scene Eight

Up the Road

(Music transitions. A bus is somehow theatrically put together on stage.)

[MUSIC NO. 08 – RIDE UP THE ROAD (GUATEMALA)]

THE NARRATOR.
> AND LIKE THAT, JUST LIKE THAT REINA IS LEAVING THE GREY
> TAKING IN THE COLORS OF A NEW DAY
> LEAVING THE ONLY PLACE SHE'S EVER KNOWN
> THROWN OUT THE OLD, TO EXPLORE NEW ZONES AND FEELING GROWN
> LIKE A GIRL NOW BECOMING A WOMAN ON HER OWN.
> PASSING PLACES THROUGH THE WINDOW, AS AN INTRO TO HAVE HER MIND BLOWN.
> AND REALIZING NOW THAT SHE'S ALL ALONE.
> AND FEAR OF THE UNKNOWN BEGINS TO SETTLE IN TO CHANGE HER TONE.
> "WHAT HAS SHE DONE? THE COOP SHE'S FLOWN.
> NOW SHE'S SO FAR FROM HOME
> WITH NO IDEA OF THE PLACES SHE'LL BE FORCED TO ROAM."
> BUT PERK UP REINA, YOU'RE WORKED UP REINA
> THIS IS YOUR PATH, THIS IS YOUR CHALLENGE, THE WORLD IS YOUR ARENA.
> YOU WARRIOR PRINCESS, YOU'LL EARN YOUR NAME
> QUEEN, OF YOUR DOMAIN
> JUST RIDE, RIDE, RIDE UP THE ROAD
> STICK YOUR HAND OUT THE WINDOW AND FEEL THE AIR FLOW
> RIDE, RIDE, RIDE UP THE ROAD
> TO THE NEXT DESTINATION, WORRY NOT ABOUT YOUR LOAD.

THE NARRATOR & REINA.
>RIDE, RIDE, RIDE UP THE ROAD
>STICK YOUR HAND OUT THE WINDOW AND FEEL THE AIR
>>FLOW

THE NARRATOR.   **REINA.**
>RIDE, RIDE, RIDE UP THE ROAD RIDE
>TO THE NEXT DESTINATION,   RIDE
>>WORRY NOT ABOUT YOUR
>>LOAD.

THE NARRATOR.
>RIDE.
>YOU'LL GET THERE, JUST RIDE.
>WHERE LIFE IS MORE FAIR, RIDE
>JUST RIDE, RIDE, RIDE UP THE ROAD!

>*(Lights transition. In a quick spotlit moment,
>we see **JULIA** finding Reina's letter.)*

>*(**JULIA** gasps.)*

Scene Nine

Guatemala

(**THE NARRATOR** *is now a* **BUS DRIVER**.)

BUS DRIVER. Welcome to *Guatemala*. If this is your final destination, well good for you. You made it to *Guatemala*. Remember to exchange your *colones* to *quetzales*. And if you will be continuing to *Tapachula, Mexico*, that bus will take off from platform B in approximately four hours. Thank you for riding with us. Now get off my bus!

REINA. Excuse me sir? Mr. Bus Driver sir?

BUS DRIVER. Yes?

REINA. I'm starving. Do you know where I could find something to eat? That long bus ride really did me in. Something not too expensive?

BUS DRIVER. Uh...yes! There's a small market down the road from here. Check it out. It's right past the bridge and past the little banana farm.

REINA. Thanks!

[MUSIC NO. 08A – INCIDENTALS]

THE NARRATOR. And off she goes. Into unfamiliar territory for the first time in her life. Reina walks just down the road, just like the handsome bus driver told her to.

> (**REINA** *takes out the Polaroid of her and baby Fernando.*)

REINA. So here we are. I'm not in *Chanmico* anymore baby boy.

THE NARRATOR. And there, beyond the bridge she sees the banana farm.

REINA. What's the harm in just taking a few? And it'll save me a *quetzal* or two.

>   (**REINA** *is about to grab a bundle of bananas off a nearby banana tree when...*)

CRUZ. Hey! What are you doing?

REINA. I uh – I –

CRUZ. You think you can just steal a hand of bananas?

REINA. I'm sorry.

CRUZ. You're more than welcome to *buy* this hand of bananas, no problem. But a hand you take a thief you make.

REINA. Absolutely. So how much for...a hand?

CRUZ. Two *quetzales*.

REINA. Okay. Here ya go.

>   (**REINA** *pays and* **CRUZ** *hands her a banana hand.*)

I'm Reina by the way. And I'm sorry again.

CRUZ. I'm Cruz. I appreciate you being honest and fair, Reina.

>   (**REINA** *scarfs down a banana.*)

There's no sense of justice with some folks anymore.

>   (**REINA** *eating fast.*)

You're pretty hungry huh?

REINA. Just haven't eaten in awhile. Been on a bus all morning.

CRUZ. Where are you from?

REINA. *El Salvador.*

CRUZ. Oh. So, what brings you to *Guatemala*?

REINA. I'm just passing through. Have a little layover.

I'm on route to the U–

> (**REINA** *catches herself.*)

–niversity.

CRUZ. University?

REINA. Yup. Uh. The one in *Mexico*. I'm...going there...to study.

CRUZ. Really?

REINA. Yeah.

CRUZ. Why *Mexico*?

REINA. Uhh...

CRUZ. Sorry. Don't mean to pry. I just think that's really interesting. I always dreamed of going to University myself, but out here, it's... well, it's not a great idea.

REINA. What do you mean?

CRUZ. Out here, University students tend to...disappear.

REINA. ...I'm sorry what now?

CRUZ. Yeah. It's...um... well, without going too much into it, the government out here sees educated folks as a threat. But, man, how nice it would be to attend University if it wasn't so dangerous.

REINA. Dangerous? Then why would you want to attend?

CRUZ. Well, awhile back we had these Guatemalan University students come into our small town of *Panzós*, just east of here where I grew up. They came to learn from us, learn about our traditional ways of farming the land. But they taught me a lot too. They'd give me all sorts of books to read. I couldn't stop reading. Still can't. Made me daydream about attending University like them.

REINA. Is that why you left?

CRUZ. ...no. I...uhh... Not long after the students came, word got out of our fertile lands, so larger farms started moving in. And then the government moved in and started building military camps in my town. It was crazy. And when my parents and our people went into town to ask why our land was being taken...they didn't come back. So, I ran. And this little farm isn't nearly what we had back home, but it's something. Work is work, you know.

[MUSIC NO. 09 – CRUZ]

REINA.
YOU WORK AND WORK AND WORK AND WORK AND WORK
AND SERVE AND SERVE AND SERVE TO TRY AND GET
    WHAT YOU DESERVE.

CRUZ. Exactly. Something is happening here in *Guatemala*, and most of us are just having to figure it out. Little by little.

REINA. I know that feeling.

CRUZ. But to continue my education, man, I mean, I'm not gonna lie, I'm a little jealous.

REINA. Really?

CRUZ. Oh yeah.
I ONCE HAD A LIFE WITH SO MUCH MORE PURPOSE
MY LIFE ON THE FARM,
WAS PLAIN BUT IN SERVICE,
OF THE LAND, THAT WE HAD, AND THE KNOWLEDGE
    THAT'D BEEN PASSED DOWN
BY OUR ANCESTORS, WHO HAD LIVED IN OUR TOWN
FOR YEARS AND YEARS AND YEARS AND YEARS.
AND NOW THAT IT'S GONE, NOW MY LIFE IS UPROOTED,
I'VE LOST WHAT I LOVED AND MY METHOD OF LEARNING

CRUZ.
>BUT I THINK THERE'S SO MUCH MORE I STILL COULD
>   ACHIEVE
>EVEN THOUGH I WAS FORCED TO LEAVE
>I COULD TAKE WHAT MY PARENTS TAUGHT ME
>AND THEIR TEACHINGS COULD LIVE THROUGH ME.
>CUZ THE LAND THAT WAS OURS,
>I WILL NO LONGER INHERIT
>BUT THE THING THAT'S STILL MINE,
>ARE MY FAMILY'S METHODS,
>AND IF I HAD A DEGREE,
>FROM A PROPER UNIVERSITY
>I COULD START FROM WHERE MY PARENTS LEFT ME
>AND READ AND READ AND READ AND READ
>ABOUT THE PLANTING OF A SEED
>AND CONTINUE, MY FAMILY'S LEGACY.

REINA. Okay I'm not supposed to tell anyone. But you seem trustworthy and not like someone who would deport me. I'm heading somewhere where you could get an education like that.

CRUZ. Yeah *Mexico*. You don't have to rub it in my face.

REINA. No. *(Beat.)* Somewhere a degree like that could get you even further! The USA!

CRUZ. What?

REINA. That's right.

I am going to America. I've heard…

[MUSIC NO. 10 – IN THE USA (MINI REPRISE)]

HOW BEAUTIFUL THAT LIFE IS!
IN THE USA, IT SEEMS LIKE LIFE IS ENDLESS
IN THE USA, YOU CAN JUST FEEL IT IN THE AIR
OUT THERE, IT FEELS LIKE LIFE IS A BIT MORE FAIR.
IN THE USA. IN THE USA.

A PLACE WHERE YOU CAN STUDY, AND READ BOOKS ALL
DAY
SOMETHING SO FAR-FETCHED HERE, IS THE AMERICAN
WAY.

CRUZ. I've actually read a lot about America's new advancements in agricultural technology.

REINA. You see!

CRUZ. So how are you getting there? On the bus?

REINA. I'm taking the bus to meet *El Gran Coyote de Tijuana*. He knows the best way into the USA and has all the answers. I'm sure he could get you an American degree too.

CRUZ. I love it! Let's go!

REINA. Oh wait, I should tell you, it costs one thousand five hundred pesos to get to *El Gran Coyote*.

CRUZ. Great let's go! I got no reason to stay here anymore. I'm in.

REINA. You have that much money?

CRUZ. There are three buses that pull in from *El Salvador* to *Guatemala* every day. You think you're the only person who makes this banana farm their first stop? Please! I've been slinging bananas for months now. Everyday. Three times a day. Seven days a week. Three hundred and sixty-five days a year. Eight thousand, seven hundred and sixty –

REINA. Okay! I get it! Just make sure not to tell anyone what we are doing? We can't get caught.

CRUZ. Deal! So? When's this bus pulling out?

REINA. In a couple of hours.

CRUZ. Okay! Let me just pack up some bananas for the road.

THE NARRATOR. All aboard! Next stop, *Tapachula, Mexico*!

[MUSIC NO. 11 – RIDE UP THE ROAD (TAPACHULA)]

JUST RIDE, RIDE, RIDE UP THE ROAD

STICK YOUR HAND OUT THE WINDOW AND FEEL THE AIR
  FLOW

RIDE, RIDE, RIDE UP THE ROAD

TO THE NEXT DESTINATION, WORRY NOT ABOUT YOUR
  LOAD.

JUST

REINA, CRUZ & THE NARRATOR.

RIDE, RIDE, RIDE UP THE ROAD

STICK YOUR HAND OUT THE WINDOW AND FEEL THE AIR
  FLOW

THE NARRATOR.	**REINA & CRUZ.**
RIDE, RIDE, RIDE UP THE ROAD	RIDE
TO THE NEXT DESTINATION, WORRY NOT ABOUT YOUR LOAD.	RIDE
RIDE.	
YOU'LL GET THERE, JUST RIDE.	
WHERE LIFE IS MORE FAIR, RIDE	
JUST RIDE, RIDE, RIDE UP THE ROAD!	

  (Transition.)

Scene Ten

What I Know

(**JULIA** *is lit with baby Fernando.*)

[MUSIC NO. 12 – WHAT I KNOW]

JULIA.
SHE'S LEFT US, SHE'S GONE.
IT'S YOU AND ME NOW, MY PRETTY LITTLE ONE.
HERE'S WHAT I KNOW
PEOPLE LEAVE. BELIEVE THAT FLEEING IS THE WAY TO GO.
ABANDON THEIR CONNECTION TO THE LAND
DON'T GIVE A SHIT THEY QUIT ON THEIR COUNTRY AND
    THEIR FELLOW MAN
SOME PEOPLE NEED A VISIT TO THE HOLY CHURCH
PRAY WITH THE BLESSED WATER AND SEE GOD'S PLAN
    WORK.
BUT WE MUST HONOR THE LIFE WE WERE GIVEN
APPRECIATE OUR EV'RY BREATH
THE WORLD MAKES ONE SINGLE PROMISE
AND THAT PROMISE ... IS DEATH

NOW I MUST BE, YOUR PARENT NOW AND RAISE YOU WELL
I NEED TO RAISE YOU LIKE I BORE YOU MYSELF.
AND LET US PRAY
LET US PRAY YOUR MOM'S DELIVERED BACK SOME WAY
GOD, LISTEN TO A WORRIED MOTHER
BRING MY DAUGHTER BACK, ONE WAY OR ANOTHER.
EVEN IF IT'S FORCEFUL, EVEN IF SHE'S DRAGGED.
PLEASE SEND FOR THEM TO BRING HER BACK ...
USE YOUR POWERS ALMIGHTY
BRING MY DAUGHTER BACK, ALIVE PLEASE!
OH! WHAT A WORLD, WHAT A WORLD.

Scene Eleven

Tapachula, Mexico

(The bus stops. **CRUZ** *and* **REINA** *are both asleep. There's a knock on the window.* **THE NARRATOR** *is now a* **MEXICAN OFFICIAL**.*)*

MEXICAN OFFICIAL. Passports?

*(**REINA** and **CRUZ** wake up and scramble to take out their documentation.)*

REINA. Here you are.

MEXICAN OFFICIAL. Where are you two off to?

REINA. Mexico City sir.

MEXICAN OFFICIAL. What's the purpose of your travels?

REINA. To study.

MEXICAN OFFICIAL. Where?

REINA. The big...University there.

MEXICAN OFFICIAL. Hmm. And what are you studying there?

REINA. Uhhh...uhm –

CRUZ. Agriculture sir.

REINA & MEXICAN OFFICIAL. What?

CRUZ. Agriculture. We are going to attend The National University of Mexico this fall. Reina and I here come from small towns where our methodology behind harvesting our crop has been passed down for centuries. Now with advancements in technology and new studies in seed germination, we are both interested in the synthesis of both ancient and modern schools of thought.

(There's a long-ass pause.)

MEXICAN OFFICIAL. Great! Welcome to *Mexico*.

CRUZ. Thank you. And would you care for a banana or two?

*(**CRUZ** takes a few bananas out of his bag.)*

MEXICAN OFFICIAL. *(Excited like a monkey.)* Ooh! Ooh! Yes! Thanks!

CRUZ. No problem. *(Under his breath.)* Now fly away.

*(The **MEXICAN OFFICIAL** exits. **REINA** and **CRUZ** get off the bus.)*

REINA. Well done.

CRUZ. Thanks. Reading books pays off every now and again.

REINA. You saved us.

CRUZ. It's no big deal.

So what now boss?

REINA. We need to find a place to spend the night. The long bus ride from here to *Guadalajara* takes off tomorrow morning.

CRUZ. *Sí pues.* Umm... well let's walk.

[MUSIC NO. 12A – TRANSITION TO SILVANO'S INN]

THE NARRATOR. And as they walk down the road, they find a quiet little inn and step inside.

*(Transition to the inside of **SILVANO**'s inn. He sits behind a desk. Grumpy. A bottle of tequila is next to him.)*

SILVANO. Hello. Welcome to Silvano's Inn. I'm Silvano. How may I help you?

REINA. Hello sir. I'm Reina. This here is Cruz.

CRUZ. Greetings!

REINA. I've been traveling for nearly 500 kilometers and haven't had a bed to sleep in since I left. We are both terribly exhausted. Might you have room for us tonight?

SILVANO. Y'all have money?

CRUZ & REINA. Of course.

SILVANO. Okay. One room will be fifty pesos a night.

REINA. Oh no sir! It'll be two. We aren't together.

CRUZ. I mean, we are together, but not together, together. Ya know?

REINA & CRUZ. Right.

SILVANO. Ah. I see. You are just friends. Not lovers.

REINA. Correct.

SILVANO. Yes. That's wise. Lovers and significant others can be *un gran dolor de cabeza*.

REINA. They sure can.

CRUZ. I guess I wouldn't know. Never had a special somebody.

SILVANO. Oh well you're a pretty lucky virgin.

CRUZ. I'm not a virgin!

SILVANO. No heartbreak. No broken promises. No children ripped away from you.

REINA. Jesus.

CRUZ. Well, they say it's better to have loved and lost than to have never loved at all.

SILVANO. They say that?

CRUZ. Yeah.

SILVANO. Who says that?

CRUZ. Well Alfred Tennyson did sir.

> (**SILVANO** *thinks about it.*)

SILVANO. Alfredo Tennyson?

CRUZ. Yup.

SILVANO. *Qué pendejo.* He was probably a virgin too.

CRUZ. I'm not a virgin!

SILVANO. My heart has been broken for a long time now and I don't see any benefits.

REINA. Who broke your heart?

SILVANO. My wife. My kids.

REINA. I'm so sorry.

SILVANO. They left me.

REINA. Why?

SILVANO. They moved to Pittsburgh, Pennsylvania. In the USA.

> (**CRUZ** *and* **REINA** *look at each other and smile.*)

What are you smiling about?! I'm telling you about my broken heart! Is this funny to you guys?!

CRUZ. No. It's just – that's where we're going!

REINA. Cruz?!

CRUZ. Oh, it's fine. He won't tell.

We're going to the USA!

We've heard…

[MUSIC NO. 12B – IN THE USA (FINAL REPRISE)]

CRUZ.

 HOW BEAUTIFUL THAT LIFE IS!

 IN THE USA, IT SEEMS LIKE LIFE IS –

SILVANO. Stop singing! I don't want to hear that!

My wife and kids sang a similar tune. Talked about how life in the States could offer much more than this. That I could open a big fancy Holiday Inn in the States. Said that I could be much more of a man than I am now. Can you imagine hearing that from your wife and kids? I know this place isn't much...but I thought it could be something. I became a man the moment I left home and decided to start my own business.

[MUSIC NO. 13 – SILVANO]

SO, I SAID I WOULDN'T GO.

I SAID NO. I PUT MY FOOT DOWN

BUT YEARS WENT ON AND THEY WOULD ASK

AND ASK AGAIN, TO LEAVE THIS SMALL TOWN,

AND I WOULD KEEP SAYING NO BUT THEY GOT RESTLESS

I WOULD ATTEMPT TO MAKE IT BETTER THOUGH HOW
 HELPLESS

SO THEN ONE DAY, THEY PACKED THEIR BAGS

SAID THEY WOULD LEAVE WITH ME OR NOT AND NOT
 COME BACK

SO, I TOLD THEM THEN TO GO!

I SAID LEAVE, OUT OF FRUSTRATION.

I GUESS I DIDN'T THINK IT THROUGH,

BUT I DON'T APPROVE, OF ULTIMATUMS

AND IN THAT MOMENT I DECIDED MY WHOLE FATE

I DIDN'T KNOW THAT'D BE THE LAST I'D SEE THEIR FACE

AND AS THE YEARS GO ON, I REALLY MISS THEM

I THINK OF ALL THE DAYS THAT I HAVEN'T KISSED THEM

FIVE YEARS NOW SINCE WE'VE BEEN APART

THEY TOOK THEIR BAGS, AND THEY TOOK MY HEART.

REINA. I'm sorry.

SILVANO. Thank you.

REINA. You know I just left my family too. My little son Fernando. See?

> (**REINA** *takes out the Polaroid and shows it to* **SILVANO.**)

SILVANO. He's so young. How could you just leave him?

REINA. Because I'm going in search of a better life for *him*. For us. And I will be back for him. I think your wife and kids had a point. The USA really can offer you much more. You started something here. Think of what you could do out there.

> (**SILVANO** *hands the picture back.*)

CRUZ. I'm going to get a degree. Learn some advanced farming techniques.

SILVANO. Good for both of you.

REINA. So, you just didn't go with them because you were too stubborn about your struggling business?

SILVANO. Excuse me?

REINA. Sounds like you let them leave because they hurt your feelings.

SILVANO. They did!

REINA. Is that a good enough reason to let five years go by without seeing them? And maybe! They weren't the problem. *(Looks at the bottle.)*

> (**SILVANO** *is silent.*)

CRUZ. Do you talk / to them still?

SILVANO. Of course. We talk on the phone. / We write letters.

REINA. Oh, that's good!

SILVANO. No, it isn't. They spend the whole time trying to convince me to come to Pittsburgh but...

REINA. But you're still holding a grudge?

SILVANO. No! I just... I don't know. They just up and left me.

REINA. You said they gave you years before they left. And it sounds like they want to see you still. They love you.

(*They all sit in silence.*)

SILVANO. Alright enough of this. How many nights do you need the rooms for?

CRUZ. We'll leave tomorrow morning.

REINA. We'll check out early and head for the bus to *Guadalajara*.

SILVANO. Y'all have a plan from there?

REINA. Yup. We're off to meet...

[MUSIC NO. 13A – EL GRAN COYOTE REPRISE]

EL GRAN COYOTE DE TIJUANA
HE'S THE ONE THAT YOU NEED WHEN YOU WANNA ...

SILVANO.
GO.

REINA. You know him??

SILVANO. Of course. He helped my family across.

CRUZ. Whaaaaa?!

SILVANO. Yes.

REINA. We hear he knows the way and has all the answers! I'm sure he could help you reconnect with your family if you needed him to.

SILVANO. What I need is 100 pesos for the rooms.

REINA. *(Dejected.)* Oh. Okay. Here you are.

   (**REINA** *and* **CRUZ** *pay.*)

[MUSIC NO. 14 – DREAM (TAPACHULA)]

SILVANO. Rooms two and four are up the stairs and to the left. See you in the morning.

   Sweet dreams.

	COMPANY EXCEPT LEONA.
THE NARRATOR.	AH
DREAM, DREAM, DREAM, DREAM,	AH
THE ONE THING WE ALL NEED TO KEEP SWIMMING UPSTREAM.	
DREAM, DREAM, DREAM, DREAM	AH
DREAM OF BETTER LIVES THOUGH HOW FAR-FETCHED IT SEEMS	
	AH

The following morning, when Reina and Cruz come down to check out...

   (**SILVANO** *stands by the doors with bags.*)

SILVANO. Good morning.

REINA & CRUZ. Good morning.

CRUZ. What is that?

SILVANO. That's my knife.

   And I don't leave home without it. *(Smiling.)*

REINA. Wait, are you coming with us?

SILVANO. Yup. I couldn't sleep last night. Thinking about what you said to me. And you're right. I need them. And I am the only person getting in the way of myself. And the people who I love.

REINA. This is exciting news! But what about your inn?

SILVANO. I sold it. To this guy. *(Points to* **THE NARRATOR***, who is now* **RODRIGO***.)* He's my neighbor Rodrigo.

RODRIGO. I'm hith neighbor Rodrigo.

SILVANO. I told him I had decided to leave and he bought it.

REINA. Great! Congrats.

RODRIGO. Thankth! I'll probably turn thith plathe into a dithco. *(Translation: Thanks! I'll probably turn this place into a disco.)*

REINA. Good for you!

Well then, we better get going! The bus is leaving soon! And remember. We have to keep our intentions under wraps.

CRUZ. Got it.

SILVANO. Let's go! I'm ready this time.

CRUZ. Let's do it!

[MUSIC NO. 14A – RIDE UP THE ROAD (GUADALAJARA)]

THE NARRATOR. What a crew!

> JUST RIDE, RIDE, RIDE UP THE ROAD
> STICK YOUR HAND OUT THE WINDOW AND FEEL THE AIR FLOW
> RIDE, RIDE, RIDE UP THE ROAD
> TO THE NEXT DESTINATION, WORRY NOT ABOUT YOUR LOAD.

REINA, CRUZ, SILVANO & THE NARRATOR.

RIDE, RIDE, RIDE UP THE ROAD
STICK YOUR HAND OUT THE WINDOW AND FEEL THE AIR
   FLOW

THE NARRATOR.	**REINA, CRUZ & SILVANO.**
RIDE, RIDE, RIDE UP THE ROAD	RIDE
TO THE NEXT DESTINATION, WORRY NOT ABOUT YOUR LOAD.	RIDE
RIDE.	
YOU'LL GET THERE, JUST RIDE.	
WHERE LIFE IS MORE FAIR, RIDE	
JUST RIDE, RIDE, RIDE UP THE ROAD!	

Scene Twelve

Guadalajara

THE NARRATOR. Ah the beautiful Mexican countryside. They ride the bus most of the day and as the sun sets, they arrive in the hustle and bustle of *Guadalajara*!

(*As* **BUS DRIVER**.) Welcome to *Guadalajara*! The current temperature is hot! And local time doesn't matter, nobody's on time anyway! Your next bus is supposed to leave in ten minutes but it probably won't leave until tomorrow! So, hope you make *limonada* out of these *limones, cabrones*!

CRUZ. Look at this place!

SILVANO. My ass hurts.

CRUZ. Yeah? I'm feeling pretty good. Limber.

SILVANO. You're young. When you get to my age your whole body stiffens up.

But some tequila should oil me right up.

REINA. We should probably find a place to get some rest for the night before you start drinking. The bus to *Tijuana* takes off bright and early tomorrow. Come on. Let's go.

[MUSIC NO. 14B – GUADALAJARA INCIDENTAL]

THE NARRATOR. And as they walk through the city streets, they pass by so many everyday folks. In everyday cars. Living everyday lives. And come across a not so everyday nun.

> (**LEONA** *is dressed in full nun garb. She is fixing the sign outside of her church.*)

REINA. Hello sister.

LEONA. Bless you children.

REINA. Thank you, sister. Might you be able to help us?

LEONA. Lord knows that I'll try.

CRUZ. We've been on a rickety old bus for nearly thirty hours. Our backs are suffering. We're looking for a place to stay tonight.

SILVANO. And a drink.

REINA. But a bed first! Just somewhere we can rest our heads until our bus departs tomorrow morning.

LEONA. You're leaving just as fast as you came in!

De dónde vienen?

CRUZ. I'm Cruz from *Guatemala*.

SILVANO. The name's Silvano. I'm from *Tapachula*.

REINA. Hi. I'm Reina. From *El Salvador*.

LEONA. Oh dear. You are all such a long way from home. Hello, my name is Sister Leona. Welcome to *Guadalajara*. And where are you all off to in the morning?

CRUZ. School! In *Tijuana*.

(**CRUZ** *shoots* **REINA** *a thumbs up.*)

LEONA. Oh yes. *Tijuana*. Yes, I've been there many times.

CRUZ. You have?

LEONA. Oh yes.

REINA. Why's that?

LEONA. Uhh... I don't like this story.

CRUZ. Well, now you have to tell us.

(**LEONA** *sighs, reaches into her pocket and takes out a flask. She takes a swig. Then hands the flask to* **SILVANO**.)

SILVANO. Much obliged.

[MUSIC NO. 15 – LEONA]

LEONA.

I'M A NUN. CLEARLY
AND MY DEVOTION TO GOD I HOLD DEARLY.
I'M ONE WHO KNEW WHAT I WOULD DO WHEN I WAS
     VERY YOUNG.
I WANTED BE A ROCK STAR, IN A ROCK 'N ROLL BAND.
BUT MY PARENTS HAD ANOTHER PLAN.
TO MARRY ME OFF TO A VERY RICH MAN.
AND I WAS LIKE, NO, NO, NO, NO, NO.
AND I WAS PUNISHED FOR THAT,
SO, I DID THE SIGN OF THE CROSS TO SHOW
I HAD A DIFF'RENT PATH
JOINED THIS CONVENT TWO WEEKS LATER AND SAT
     AMONG
SOME OF THE BRIGHTEST, WISEST, BADDEST BITCHES IN
     CHURCHES LEFT UNSUNG

CRUZ. *(Aside.)* Can she say that?

LEONA.

WOMEN WHO SHOWED ME THE LIGHT, WHO SHOWED ME
     THE WAY TO BE,
UNBEKNOWNST TO THEM, THESE SISTERS SAVED ME
BUT I STILL WANT TO BE A ROCK STAR, IN A ROCK AND
     ROLL BAND
I WANT TO GO TO THE ROCK AND ROLL MECCA, BUT I
     DON'T THINK I CAN

REINA. Why not? Is it too far?

LEONA.

IT'S IN THE USA.

SILVANO. That's where we are going!!

CRUZ. By way of *Tijuana*.

REINA. You guys!

LEONA.
SEE HERE'S THE THING, I'VE BEEN.
TRIED TO CROSS ON MY VERY OWN
I'VE GONE FOUR TIMES, LEFT HERE, SEEN THE BORDER,
    CHICKENED OUT AND COME HOME
MAYBE IT'S GOD, MAYBE IT'S ME,
MAYBE IT'S THE DANGER
MAYBE I'M TOO COWARDLY,
BUT I WISH I WAS A ROCK STAR, LIKE JANIS JOPLIN OR
    JOAN JETT
BUT I'M AFRAID OF THE DREAM THAT I WANT AND BEING
    PUNISHED AGAIN
CUZ GOD AND THESE LADIES SAVED ME FROM A LIFE
    I DIDN'T WANT
SO, I'M AFRAID OF LEAVING THEM HERE, LEAVING FOR
    AMERICA, AND CHASING MY SONG.
YEAH!

CRUZ. Just chase it sister!

SILVANO. Yeah. You've got a great voice!

LEONA. Oh stop.

CRUZ. No really!

LEONA. Listen, I've had men try to take advantage of me my entire life. I have an awful relationship with my parents. I fought off marrying a grizzly old man.

REINA. Jesus! *(Catches herself.)*

LEONA. Yup! Him too. I'm scared of him the most. And all I have left is a little song in my heart.

CRUZ. Well... I'm sure *El Gran Coyote de Tijuana* can help you too! I mean, I don't know about striking a record deal but I'm sure he could guide you to –

LEONA. Cleveland? The home of rock and roll?

REINA. Maybe.

LEONA. Who is this *Gran Coyote* you speak of?

CRUZ. Oh, you don't know him? Maybe that's why you didn't make it any of those other times!

SILVANO. He helped my family cross. I'm hoping he can help me get to them.

CRUZ. He's gonna help me get an American degree!

REINA. And he's going to help me find a new home.

LEONA. You think he could help me grow some *cojones* and finally make it across?

REINA. Yes! Come with us!

LEONA. You'll hold my hand?

> (**LEONA** *extends her hand.* **REINA** *takes ahold of her hand.*)

REINA. Of course.

LEONA. Bless you.

CRUZ. You need one thousand five hundred pesos though. For *El Gran Coyote*.

LEONA. Oh, that won't be a problem. This is a Catholic church. We have all the money. They won't miss it.

CRUZ. Oh right.

SILVANO. Perfect! We'll pick you up in the morning! Now papa has to lie down. Did you say you knew of an inn somewhere around here?

LEONA. I do. But you should stay here. Save your pesos children.

CRUZ. Really?

REINA. We won't be an inconvenience?

LEONA. Of course not! We open our church for all who need a roof over their heads. Come on in!

THE NARRATOR. And boom! Just like that the group has found their last place to stay before the last bus to glory in the morning.

[MUSIC NO. 16 – DREAM (GUADALAJARA)]

	COMPANY.
THE NARRATOR.	AH
DREAM, DREAM, DREAM, DREAM,	
THE ONE THING WE ALL NEED TO	
KEEP SWIMMING UPSTREAM.	
DREAM, DREAM, DREAM, DREAM	
DREAM OF BETTER LIVES THOUGH	AH
HOW FAR-FETCHED IT SEEMS	
	AH

THE NARRATOR. That night, as they are all beginning to sleep one last sleep before the big day, Reina asks Cruz to borrow a blank page from one of his books.

(**REINA** *sits up to write a letter.*)

REINA. Dear Mama Julia, I know you must be mad at me, but I'm enclosing a vial of holy water from a church in *Guadalajara*. So, you know I'm safe with God. Let it melt your worries away. Give Fernando a kiss for me. Love, Reina.

(*In a pool of light, we see* **JULIA** *and Fernando receive the letter.*)

Scene Thirteen

Off to Meet El Coyote

THE NARRATOR.   The following morning, the crew is complete!! All aboard! Bus bound for *Tijuana*, Let's get it!

> (**REINA** *grabs ahold of* **LEONA***'s hand and squeezes it tight.*)

[MUSIC NO. 17 – RIDE UP THE ROAD (TIJUANA)]

OFF THEY GO! HERE WE GO,

ONE AND A TWO AND A THREE ONE MORE MAKES IT FO'

ON THE BUS TO THE BORDER

THEY KEEP CHUGGING ALONG MAKING THE TRIP TO
    BETTER LIVES SHORTER

TIJUANA COMES NEXT,

ALL OF THEM EXCITED BUT STILL WITH A DEEP FEAR IN
    THEIR CHEST

ON THE QUEST FOR EL GRAN COYOTE

DREAMING THE IMPOSSIBLE DREAM LIKE DON QUIXOTE

THEY HOLD EACH OTHER TIGHT

TO MAKE IT SEEM ALRIGHT

CUZ THEY ARE ON THEIR WAY TO THE FINISH LINE FIGHT

AND WELL ON THEIR WAY TO MEET THE WIZARD

WHEN DAY TURNS TO NIGHT.

JUST RIDE, RIDE, RIDE UP THE ROAD

STICK YOUR HAND OUT THE WINDOW AND FEEL THE AIR
    FLOW

RIDE, RIDE, RIDE UP THE ROAD

TO THE NEXT DESTINATION, WORRY NOT ABOUT YOUR
    LOAD.

JUST

THE NARRATOR.

RIDE, RIDE, RIDE UP THE ROAD

STICK YOUR HAND OUT THE WINDOW AND FEEL THE AIR FLOW

RIDE, RIDE, RIDE UP THE ROAD

TO THE NEXT DESTINATION, WORRY NOT ABOUT YOUR LOAD.

REINA, CRUZ, SILVANO & LEONA.

RIDE, RIDE, RIDE UP THE ROAD

STICK YOUR HAND OUT THE WINDOW AND FEEL THE AIR FLOW

RIDE.

RIDE.

REINA.

YOU'LL GET THERE

WHERE LIFE IS MORE FAIR,

JUST RIDE,

RIDE, RIDE, RIDE UP THE ROAD.

CRUZ, SILVANO, LEONA & THE NARRATOR.

RIDE, RIDE, RIDE UP THE ROAD

STICK YOUR HAND OUT THE WINDOW AND FEEL THE AIR FLOW

RIDE.

RIDE.

Scene Fourteen

Red Skies

[MUSIC NO. 18 – RED SKIES]

*(Lights come up on **JULIA**, sweeping.)*

JULIA.

MAYBE I WAS WRONG
MAYBE I'M NOT STRONG ENOUGH
TO BEAR THIS PAIN
AND CARRY THIS WEIGHT.

EV'RY SINGLE DAY
MORE AND MORE RUN AWAY
AND I'M BEGINNING TO SEE
WHY REINA CHOSE TO LEAVE

TODAY I SOLD OUR BEANS MYSELF
AND SAW THAT OUR TOWN'S NOT DOING WELL
THE TROUBLE IN THE COUNTRY IS WIDELY KNOWN
NOW THAT TROUBLE IS RIPPLING SO CLOSE TO HOME

AND NOW THE SKY HAS TURNED FROM GREY TO RED.
AND I'M AFRAID THAT GOD'S HINTING AT BLOODSHED
AND I'M AFRAID FOR OUR LIVES
OR GOD FORBID THAT BLOOD IS MY CHILD'S
MY ONLY DAUGHTER

HOW CAN WE PROCEED WITH CAUTION?
EVEN IF IT'S ALL FORGIVEN, NOTHING IS FORGOTTEN
I AM SO VERY FRIGHTENED
FOR ALL THE PAIN ON THE HORIZON

HERE'S WHAT I KNOW
PEOPLE LEAVE, BELIEVE THAT FLEEING IS THE WAY TO GO.
ABANDON THEIR CONNECTION TO THE LAND
THEY DON'T CONSIDER THE HARDSHIP OF LOSING A
    HELPING HAND

SO, I WILL PRAY
I WILL PRAY THAT WE SURVIVE HERE, CUZ WE STAYED
CUZ NOW I HAVE NO CHOICE
I'M STUCK JUST ME AND MY BOYS.
ME AND MY OFFSPRING, THEY ARE MY EV'RYTHING
I WON'T GO ANYWHERE, OR DO ANYTHING
BUT PRAY
I'LL PRAY THAT I SEE MY GIRL BACK HERE SOME DAY
AND I WILL HONOR THE LIFE I WAS GIVEN
APPRECIATE MY EV'RY BREATH
CUZ THE WORLD MAKES ONE SINGLE PROMISE
AND THAT PROMISE ...

CUZ THE SKY HAS TURNED FROM GREY TO RED.
AND I'M AFRAID GOD'S HINTING AT BLOODSHED
I'M AFRAID FOR MY LIFE
AND YET I PRAY YOU'D TAKE MINE BEFORE YOU TAKE MY
    CHILD'S.

THE SKY DOESN'T LIE
LORD, PLEASE BE KIND.

Scene Fifteen

Tijuana

BUS DRIVER. Welcome to *Tijuana*! You made it! Where the drinking age is eighteen and prostitution is legal! *(Winks at audience member.)* Have fun!

(The bus takes off into the night.)

CRUZ. Look at us! We made it!

SILVANO. *Tijuana.*

LEONA. What time is it?

SILVANO. Eight p.m.

CRUZ. So now what?

REINA. ...

SILVANO. Where are we off to now?

REINA. Uhm. I don't know.

CRUZ. What do you mean?

REINA. I guess I didn't ask. Don Napo just said to get on the bus to *Tijuana* and *El Gran Coyote* would be here.

SILVANO. Who is Don Napo?

REINA. My old boss.

LEONA. Has he made this journey?

REINA. I don't think so, no.

CRUZ. Oh no.

REINA. But he knows of many friends who have!

LEONA. So, what should we do now dear? It's dark and we'll probably need to –

(All of a sudden there is a flash of light! It's so bright. It blinds **REINA**, **CRUZ**, **SILVANO**, *and* **LEONA**. *It's the bright headlights from a pickup truck. The engine roars!)*

[MUSIC NO. 18A – COYOTE THE WIZARD]

EL GRAN COYOTE DE TIJUANA. COME FORWARD!

REINA. It's him! We're here!

EL GRAN COYOTE. WHOOOOOO ARE YOU?!

REINA. It is us. Reina!

CRUZ. And Cruz!

SILVANO. And Silvano!

> *(***LEONA*** has hidden behind* **SILVANO**. **SILVANO** *steps aside to reveal* **LEONA**.*)*

LEONA. And me. Leona.

EL GRAN COYOTE. WHAT HAS BROUGHT YOU HERE?!

REINA. We are in search of the one they call *El Gran Coyote de Tijuana.*

EL GRAN COYOTE. And who is he?

REINA, CRUZ & SILVANO.
HE'S THE ONE THAT YOU NEED WHEN YOU WANNA ... GO!

EL GRAN COYOTE. Ah yes! Then yooooooooou have arrived to the right place.

AND WHAT IS IT YOU WANT?!

CRUZ. I'm in search of an American Degree. From a prestigious University.

SILVANO. I need to reconnect with my family in the States. That you helped across many years ago.

REINA. I'm looking for a new home in the USA where I can provide my son with the life he deserves.

EL GRAN COYOTE. *(To* **LEONA.***)* And you?

LEONA. I want be a rock star? In a rock and roll band? But on second thought, there's a baptism I'm missing so I'm gonna scoot.

(**LEONA** *starts to leave.)*

EL GRAN COYOTE. YOOOOOOUUUUU STAAAAAAAY!

(**LEONA** *freezes.* **REINA** *grabs her by the hand.)*

Do you have the money I require?

REINA. Oh yes!

(**REINA** *collects the money from the others. They lay it on the floor in front of them. The engine turns off. The lights turn off.* **THE NARRATOR** *appears in a cowboy hat as* **EL GRAN COYOTE DE TIJUANA.** *He's pretty normal looking but has a heavy Texas drawl, with the cool swagger of Clint Eastwood, and the explosive confidence of Yosemite Sam.)*

EL GRAN COYOTE. Good. I'll take that.

(**EL GRAN COYOTE** *picks up the money and counts it.)*

So!

Y'all ready?

CRUZ. Ready as ever.

EL GRAN COYOTE. Well alright. So, the desert is just behind us. You'll be traveling through the desert for as long as it takes. Could be a few nights. You CANNOT walk during the day. You'll be too easy to spot and that sun'll cook ya. So, you walk at night. Avoid the helicopters. They fly all throughout the day, but those first few miles near *Tijuana* they buzz around like bees. Anytime you see cactus, refuel.

SILVANO. Refuel?

EL GRAN COYOTE. Yes. You'll find that cactuses –

CRUZ. Cacti.

EL GRAN COYOTE. I'm sorry?

CRUZ. Cacti. The plural word for cactus.

> *(Beat.)*

EL GRAN COYOTE. This kid serious?

REINA. Yes.

EL GRAN COYOTE. *(Sighs loudly.)* You'll find that *cacti* *(Pronounced cack-tea.)* plants have water inside them, cut them open and use them to replenish nutrients.

SILVANO. No problem. I brought my knife.

EL GRAN COYOTE. Beyond that, a new world awaits.

REINA. Wait you won't be coming with us?

EL GRAN COYOTE. Oh no. I will meet you on the other side.

REINA. But –

EL GRAN COYOTE. No buts! Take advantage of the nights. And remember, do not get caught. If you get caught, do not try to run. They got no issues shooting you dead. So, if you are caught, well bust my buttons... You will be arrested, and if you are lucky, you will be sent back home...eventually. You will lose all the money and if you choose to try again, you will have to repay me because I will not remember you. I meet thousands of people. I'm a very popular guy. Understood? Great. Grand. Good Luck!

> *(**EL GRAN COYOTE** gets back into the truck and it roars off.)*

CRUZ. That's the guy we were all so excited to meet?

SILVANO. We paid all that money for that?

LEONA. Very underwhelming indeed.

(**REINA** *looks at the money she has left.*)

REINA. I barely have any money left now. I wonder how much this'll be in American dollars.

(**THE NARRATOR** *reapproaches as a* **MEXICAN IMMIGRATION OFFICIAL**.)

MEXICAN OFFICIAL. I'm sorry what did you say miss?? ... What did you say?

REINA. I'm sorry?

MEXICAN OFFICIAL. Did I just hear you ask about American currency?

...Miss?

Are you all planning on making a move into the desert to cross into the United States illegally?

...

CRUZ. No.

MEXICAN OFFICIAL. Then why would she ask that question?

SILVANO. Uhh...

MEXICAN OFFICIAL. I'll ask you again miss, (*To* **REINA**.) are you planning on illegally crossing into the U.S.?

REINA. No.

MEXICAN OFFICIAL. Are you from *Tijuana*?

REINA. Yes.

MEXICAN OFFICIAL. May I see some documentation proving that you are?

...

Or from any of you?

…

No?

…

Well then you are all under arrest.

…

(Into radio.) Aquí tengo cuatro dilencuentes cerca de la frontera. Necesito refuerzos.

LEONA. God forgive me!!

[MUSIC NO. 18B – KICK IN THE BALLS]

*(**LEONA** takes her head piece veil and throws it over the **MEXICAN OFFICIAL**'s head and hits him in the balls.)*

Run!!

(The crew quickly runs away.)

MEXICAN OFFICIAL. Hey! Hey! I need backup! We have four illegals heading into the desert, trying to cross into the United States. I need backup damnit! Now!

*(The **MEXICAN OFFICIAL** runs off.)*

Scene Sixteen

Through the Desert

REINA. Thank you, Sister!

LEONA. I don't know what came over me.

REINA. I'm so sorry I opened my big mouth! I can't believe I nearly ruined this for all of us.

SILVANO. Don't worry about it. What's done is done.

CRUZ. We better move fast. Now they know what we look like.

SILVANO. We better hurry.

[MUSIC NO. 19 – DESERT (PART 1)]

(The sound of buzzing helicopters.)

CRUZ. The helicopters.

REINA. Already?

>   *(**REINA**, **CRUZ**, **SILVANO**, and **LEONA** kneel together.)*

LEONA. *Santa María,*

   Madre de Dios,

REINA, CRUZ, SILVANO & LEONA. *ruega por nosotros los pecadores,*

   ahora y en la hora de nuestra muerte.

SILVANO. Let's get a move on!

THE NARRATOR. *Día Uno. Esperanza.*

SILVANO.

Se me fueron.
Toda mi
familia. Inez, **CRUZ**.   **LEONA**.   **REINA**.
Carmensita,   *Me mataron*   *Dios te salve,*   *Fernando,*
Florencio. Y *mis papas.*   *María,*   *te quiero*
fue mi culpa. *Me mataron*   *llena eres*   *con todo mi*
Por ser como *nuestras*   *de gracia,*   *Corazón.*
soy. Y aquí   *tradiciones.* *el Señor es*   *Te extraño*
pensando   *Pero viven en* *contigo.*   *tanto.*
que ellos eran *mi. Lo perdí*   KEEP
los culpables. *todo. Todito.*   MOVING!
Pero no. Así   *Esto es para*
no fue.   I HEAR   *ti.*
                THEIR
                GUNS!
                STAY
                DOWN!

[BREATH]   [BREATH]   [BREATH]   [BREATH]
[BREATH]   [BREATH]   [BREATH]   [BREATH]
[BREATH]   [BREATH]   [BREATH]   [BREATH]
[BREATH]   [BREATH]   [BREATH]   [BREATH]

THE NARRATOR. *Día Dos. Fe.*

(*Music slows down.*)

SILVANO.   **CRUZ**.
Horribles!   *Quiero una*   **LEONA**.   **REINA**.
Horribles   *educación*   *Bendita tú*   *Por Dios.*
los años que   *donde*   *eres entre*
han pasado.   *yo puedo*   *todas las*   *Por Dios.*
Cada noche   *honorar la*   *mujeres, y*
solo. IT'S SO   *vida de mis*   *bendito es*   *Por Dios.*
COLD!   *papas y la*   *el fruto de*
STAY   *técnica de mi*   *tu vientre,*
CLOSE!   *pueblo.*   *Jesús.*

SILVANO.	CRUZ.		REINA.
NO ONE IS FREEZING TO DEATH!!	*Sé que tengo la capacidad de usar mi cerebro.*		WE CAN MAKE IT!
		LEONA.	
[BREATH]	[BREATH]	[BREATH]	[BREATH]
[BREATH]	[BREATH]	[BREATH]	[BREATH]
[BREATH]	[BREATH]	[BREATH]	[BREATH]
[BREATH]	[BREATH]	[BREATH]	[BREATH]

THE NARRATOR. *Día Tres. Angustia.*

(Music slows down more.)

SILVANO.	CRUZ.	LEONA.	REINA.
Lo único que quiero es estar con ellos. Abrazarlos. Besarlos. Pedirles perdón. Que he cambiado y quiero ser el padre y el esposo que se merecen. Si salimos de este desierto viviré la vida para ellos. Porque ellos son mi Corazón. Ellos son todo Mi Corazón.	*Sé que lo puedo hacer. Es mi sueño. No me puedo morir en este desierto. No puedo. No puedo. No puedo.* I CAN'T! PLEASE! *Mis estudios. Mis tradiciones. Mis manos. Mi Mente. Mi cerebro.* I CAN'T! PLEASE!! I CAN'T! PLEASE!! I CAN'T! PLEASE!!	*Santa María, Madre de Dios, ruega por nosotros, pecadores, ahora y en la hora de nuestra muerte. Y si ahora es la hora de nuestra muerte??* PLEASE GOD HELP US. WE NEED WATER. THIS DESERT WILL SWALLOW US!	SOMEWHERE OVER THE BORDER SOMEWHERE WE CAN BREATHE FREE SOMEWHERE OVER THE BORDER JUST YOU AND ME [BREATH]

SILVANO.	LEONA.	REINA.
WE HAVE TO MAKE IT PAST THE MUDSLIDE!	GOD! *Por mi culpa. Por mi culpa. Por mi gran culpa. Dame poder Señor. Dame Valentía! Quítame el temor.* LEAVE ME! I'M NOT GONNA MAKE IT.	[BREATH] [BREATH] NOOOOOOOOO!

(A moment outside of time...)

REINA. Back in *Chanmico* I saw a picture of America. A beautiful house. Children standing outside near a nice white picket fence. Green grass.

I pictured my son playing in our yard in America. He looked so happy. That's what I want. The house. The fence. The happy child, running around without fear or worries. That's all I want. The perfect life.

(Then, back to reality.)

[MUSIC NO. 20 – DESERT (PART 2)]

WE'RE GONNA MAKE IT THROUGH THE DARKNESS, THROUGH THE NIGHT!

SILVANO. What?

REINA.
WE'RE GONNA MAKE IT THROUGH THE DARKNESS, THROUGH THE NIGHT!

LEONA. I just don't think I can.

REINA, CRUZ & SILVANO.
WE'RE GONNA MAKE IT THROUGH THE DARKNESS, THROUGH THE NIGHT!

REINA, CRUZ, SILVANO & LEONA.
WE'RE GONNA MAKE IT THROUGH THE DARKNESS,
THROUGH THE NIGHT!

> *(They all join hands and help* **LEONA** *across.*
> *They hug and laugh.)*

REINA. We made it!

LEONA. *Gracias a Dios!* Thank you!

CRUZ. We did it!

SILVANO. *Órale!*

> *(All of a sudden there is a flash of light again!*
> *It's bright. It blinds* **REINA**, **CRUZ**, **SILVANO**,
> *and* **LEONA**. *It's the bright headlights again.*
> *Over a megaphone we hear:)*

THE NARRATOR. FREEZE! Put your hands up where we can
see them! You are under arrest for illegal immigration!

REINA. No please!

> *(The lights and the roaring engine turn off.*
> **THE NARRATOR** *appears as* **EL GRAN COYOTE**.*)*

EL GRAN COYOTE. I'm just kidding.

SILVANO. What?

EL GRAN COYOTE. *(Hillbilly laugh.)* Congratulations.
Welcome to America!

CRUZ. Why would you do that to us?

EL GRAN COYOTE. I'm sorry. No but really. I'm proud of you.

REINA. That's messed up.

EL GRAN COYOTE. Listen little missy, I'm trying to lighten
the mood because this isn't quite the end of the journey.

LEONA. What? You mean, there's more?

EL GRAN COYOTE. Oh yes! You see you made it through the desert to the border but now we need to get you through immigration.

SILVANO. Okay?

LEONA. So, what now?

EL GRAN COYOTE. Well, you see here you got two choices. Three of you get into a mattress truck and one of you rides with me in my pickup.

CRUZ. Someone just gets to just ride with you in your truck?

EL GRAN COYOTE. Well not up front. In the back. Covered by a board. And flowers on top to mask the person.

REINA. Or a mattress truck?

EL GRAN COYOTE. Correct. I need three of you to hide in between the mattresses that are stacked in the back of the big truck.

REINA. That sounds awful.

EL GRAN COYOTE. It sure is. But no one said this would be easy.

REINA. Can we avoid immigration?

EL GRAN COYOTE. You ready to spend another three days in the desert?

　　　　(All silent.)

SILVANO. You ride in the pickup truck Reina.

REINA. What? No!

CRUZ. Yeah! It's gotta be you.

REINA. Why me?

LEONA. Because you brought us here together. You made all this happen. You should be the one.

REINA. No! Mr. *Coyote* I don't want to be separated from my friends.

EL GRAN COYOTE. Nothin' I can do about it. It's the way it has to be.

REINA. You guys! No.

CRUZ. Come on Reina. We are so close.

SILVANO. Just ride in the back and we will see you on the other side.

LEONA. Don't you worry about us dear.

EL GRAN COYOTE. Then it's settled. You three will ride in the mattress truck and you'll come with me.

Remember to take a nice big breath of fresh air in before you get into the trucks. Air in there is a limited supply.

(**REINA** *runs to hug her friends.*)

SILVANO. It's gonna be okay.

LEONA. Trust in God. He'll guide us.

CRUZ. See you soon.

EL GRAN COYOTE. Alright. Y'all go ahead.

(**CRUZ**, **SILVANO**, *and* **LEONA** *head for the truck and exit.*)

Scene Seventeen

Under the Flowers

EL GRAN COYOTE. Now what's your name again?

REINA. Reina.

EL GRAN COYOTE. Alright Reina. I'm gonna try to get through as fast as I can. It's gonna get hot under there, and you won't have a ton of air. But worry you not. As long as they don't ask for an inspection you won't be in there long. If they ask for an inspection, stay still and you don't make a sound. Even breathing loudly, they'll hear that. Hopefully we pass.

REINA. And if we don't?

EL GRAN COYOTE. ...

Then it's all over.

REINA. Oh my god.

EL GRAN COYOTE. You ready?

REINA. Ummm...

EL GRAN COYOTE. Good. Come on.

REINA. Mr. *Coyote*?

EL GRAN COYOTE. Yes?

REINA. You promise this will work?

> *(A very long pause.* **EL GRAN COYOTE** *decides whether to be really honest or not.)*

EL GRAN COYOTE. Sure.

[MUSIC NO. 20A – FLOWER TRUCK]

(**REINA** *gets into the back of the pickup truck.*
EL GRAN COYOTE *grabs a wooden board and
fits it on top. Then he places flower pots on
top of the board. The lighting focuses in on*
REINA *under the boards as the truck drives
off. There is no space for her to move. We
hear the car engine start and drive for a bit.*
REINA *rolls minimally as the car moves. We
watch her begin to sweat. Until finally the
car stops.* **REINA** *reaches into her pocket and
takes out the picture of her and her son. She
hears mumbled conversations between* **EL
GRAN COYOTE** *and Immigration Border
Officials. It goes on for a bit.* **REINA** *is trying
to understand and lies still. Trying not to
breathe. She wipes sweat from her brow.
Suddenly, we hear a voice say "Inspection!"
She clutches the picture close to her heart.
The conversation continues. It's inaudible.
There's tapping on all sides of the pickup
truck. A stick pokes into the flower bed all
around nearly hitting* **REINA**.)

(*Then a long silence.*)

(**REINA** *is running out of air.*)

(*Finally. Finally, we hear "All clear!"*)

(*And the truck pulls ahead.*)

(**REINA** *does the sign of the cross.*)

REINA. Thank you, God. Thank you thank you thank you.

(*She kisses the picture and the pickup truck's
engine stops. The flowers come off. The board
comes off.* **REINA** *takes an enormous gasp of
air.* **EL GRAN COYOTE** *hands her a bottle of
water. She finishes it.*)

EL GRAN COYOTE. Congratulations. You made it! San Diego, California.

REINA. Where are the others?

EL GRAN COYOTE. Not sure.

REINA. What do you mean you're not sure?

EL GRAN COYOTE. I didn't drive that truck. I drove you. I don't know if they made it through.

REINA. What?

EL GRAN COYOTE. Exactly what I said.

REINA. But you were supposed to have all the answers!

EL GRAN COYOTE. I never promised you all the answers.

REINA. But what about my friends?!

EL GRAN COYOTE. I'm sorry miss.

> (**EL GRAN COYOTE** *starts to leave.*)

REINA. Wait!

EL GRAN COYOTE. You made it. Now take it step by step. Gotta go.

> (**EL GRAN COYOTE** *gets in his pickup and drives away.*)
>
> (**REINA** *is left alone. Silence. She stands, frozen in place. Looking around. With no sense of what direction to go. Stillness.*)

Scene Eighteen

Step by Step

[MUSIC NO. 21 – STEP BY STEP]

REINA. Okay. Just wait. Wait. Breathe. Just Breathe.

STEP BY STEP, THAT'S ALL HE SAID
SO, WHAT'S MY NEXT STEP?
WHAT WILL I DO NOW, WHERE SHOULD I GO?
SOYLA SHOULD BE HERE NOW BUT I GUESS SHE DIDN'T
    SHOW.
WHAT IF, I MADE A MISTAKE
I'M THE ONLY ONE TO BLAME
I BROUGHT THIS ONTO MY VERY OWN SELF.
AND WHERE ARE THE OTHERS, DID THEY ALSO MAKE IT
    THROUGH?
I SHOULD CHECK IF THEY'RE NEAR, BUT I CAN'T MOVE.
I'M STUCK
I MADE IT HERE BUT I'M ALL ALONE AGAIN
I MADE IT HERE AND I THOUGHT THIS'D BE THE END.
BUT NOW I'M PARALYZED
I SACRIFICED
THE ONLY LIFE I KNEW
FOR A LIFE I KNOW EVEN LESS.
PLEASE BLESSED GOD, RELIEVE MY STRESS,
SHOW ME THE LIGHT AND GIVE ME STRENGTH
I HAVE TO TAKE A LITTLE STEP.

     (She can't.)

MY MOTHER, WOULD SAY I TOLD YOU SO
FERNANDO, I APOLOGIZE
I SACRIFICED
THE DAYS I'D WATCH YOU GROW
AND WHAT WILL I HAVE TO SHOW?

FOR YOU I'LL MOVE AND TAKE
ONE SMALL STEP

>*(She takes her first step. And from off we hear "REINA!"* **REINA** *looks out. "It's me! Soyla! Antonia's daughter! Get in the car! Hurry!"* **REINA**'s *face lights up!)*

Scene Nineteen

Life in America

[MUSIC NO. 22 – LIFE IN AMERICA]

REINA.
> FINALLY, I CAN BREATHE,
> SOMEONE CALLED MY NAME IN THE STATES AND GOT ME
>   TO UNFREEZE MY FEET.
> I LEAVE SAN DIEGO AND HEAD FOR L.A., WITH SOYLA, TO
>   SOYLA'S HOME
> SOYLA, THE ONLY PERSON IN THE STATES I KNOW
> AND SHE VERY GENTLY TELLS ME HOW I'LL PAY OFF
>   WHAT I OWE
> BUT FIRST SHE TAKES ME HOME AND I GET TO PLAY WITH
>   HER DAUGHTERS
> SHE SITS ME ON HER COUCH AND SHE GIVES ME A GLASS
>   OF WATER
> AND IT'S THE BEST I'VE EVER TASTED
> I ASK HER HOW SHE DID IT ALL WITH NO TIME WASTED.
> SHE TELLS ME THAT SHE WORKS AND WORKS AND
>   WORKS AND WORKS
> AND SERVES AND SERVES AND SERVES TO GET WHAT SHE
>   DESERVES.
> I TELL HER I WANT IT TOO
> AND THE VERY NEXT DAY SHE BUYS ME A MOP AND
>   BROOM
> I CLEAN THE HOUSES OF RICH FOLKS IN TOWN
> I KEEP MY HOPES HIGH AND I KEEP MY HEAD DOWN
>
> BUT SOON ENOUGH, THE FOLKS SEND ME HOME CRYING
> YELL AT ME TO LEARN ENGLISH FAST EVEN THOUGH I'M
>   REALLY TRYING
> I HEAR BEANER AND WETBACK SLIP FROM OUT THEIR
>   MOUTHS

LIKE I DON'T KNOW BETTER CUZ I'M FROM A COUNTRY
    DOWN SOUTH
THEY TREAT ME ONLY LIKE THE HELP, LIKE I'M NOT
    REALLY A HUMAN
I FEEL STUPID AND WOUNDED AND THE ILLUSION
OF THE DREAM IS RUINED.
CUZ THE SITUATION'S BAD
AND ALL I WANTED WAS A DIFF'RENT LIFE FOR MY SON
    THAN I HAD
AND THEN IT DAWNS,
'N TRUST I DON'T SAY THIS LIGHTLY,
IT SEEMS THE AMERICAN DREAM ISN'T REAL
FOR PEOPLE WHO LOOK LIKE ME.

AND I THINK ABOUT MY MOTHER,
RAISING MY LITTLE KID
KNOWING THAT SHE'S MAD FOR WHY I LEFT AND HOW
    I DID.
SO, I CALL AND WRITE AND CALL AND WRITE
TO TRY TO MAKE IT RIGHT
I CALL AND WRITE AND CALL AND WRITE
EV'RY SINGLE NIGHT.

SENDING MONEY BACK TO HELP, AND KEEPING MY EYES
    ON THE NEWS
WATCHING THE WAR RAGE, AND THE VIOLENCE THAT
    ENSUES
I APPLY FOR A GREEN CARD AND DO THE SIGN OF THE
    CROSS
KNOWING I CAN'T GO BACK OR ALL MY PROGRESS WILL
    BE LOST
SO, I CRY EV'RY NIGHT, I LIVE A LIFE WITH LITTLE JOY
I CRY EV'RY NIGHT
CUZ I'M AFRAID FOR MY BOY

    (**CRUZ**, **SILVANO**, *and* **LEONA** *all reappear
    as ghosts or dreams or figments of Reina's
    imagination.*)

CRUZ, SILVANO & LEONA. Reina!

(They wave.)

YOU MADE IT THROUGH
YOU'RE STILL ALIVE
BE GRATEFUL YOU MADE IT
YOU SURVIVED.
MAYBE WE LIVED, MAYBE WE DIED.
EITHER WAY IT WAS PROUDLY, WE TRIED
WE WENT ON THE RIDE, YOU DID US RIGHT
SO, MAKE IT THROUGH THE DARKNESS, THROUGH THE
    NIGHT
YOU'LL NEVER KNOW IT
WE MISS YOU SO MUCH
SO, LOOK TO THE SKIES
THAT'S HOW WE'LL KEEP IN TOUCH.

(They disappear. **REINA** *looks to the skies.)*

REINA.

I WILL KEEP IN TOUCH.
GOD ONLY KNOWS IF I SEE THEM AGAIN
BUT THE LIFE I HAVE, I OWE IT ALL TO THEM
AND THOSE BACK HOME WHO ALSO LENT THEIR HANDS
SO, I WILL SUCCEED HERE OR I'LL BE DAMNED

THE GRIND IS A SERIOUS THING
PROVE MYSELF BY WORK ETHIC AND THE COIN I CAN
    BRING IN
I WORK AND WORK AND WORK AND WORK AND WORK
AND SERVE AND SERVE AND SERVE TO GET WHAT
    I DESERVE
THIS WASN'T EXACTLY THE FAIRY TALE THAT I IMAGINED
THIS WASN'T THE ORIGINAL STORY,
SO, I TAKE ACTION.
I PAY OFF MY DEBT, I THANK SOYLA BUT THEN
I LEAVE CUZ I HEAR THERE'S MORE JOBS IN THE
    MIDWEST.

THAT IS WHAT I FOLLOW, END UP IN CHICAGO, WHERE I
    HAVE TO START AGAIN
AND THE WHOLE TIME, I KEEP IN MIND WHY DO IT,
FOR THAT MOMENT WHEN,
MY BOY WILL JOIN ME, IN ILLINOIS, AND WE CAN START
    IT ALL FRESH
BUT IN THE MEANTIME, I START A BUSINESS OF MY OWN.
I LEARN ENGLISH FROM SOAP OPERAS AND THE
    CHILDREN IN THE HOMES
THAT I CLEAN.

And I learn that Reina in America means Queen.

COMPANY EXCEPT REINA.
SO HOW LONG DOES IT TAKE?

REINA.
TEN YEARS!

COMPANY EXCEPT REINA.
HOW LONG DOES IT TAKE?

REINA.
TEN YEARS!

COMPANY EXCEPT REINA.
HOW LONG DOES IT TAKE?

REINA.
TEN YEARS!
TEN HARD YEARS!

'Til I can fly back...

> *(We hear the sound of an airplane flying overhead.)*

...Here.

Scene Twenty

Back Home

(We are transported back to Chanmico. **JULIA** *appears hanging clothes to dry.* **REINA** *approaches.* **JULIA** *sees her.)*

REINA. It's good to see you.

> *(**JULIA** is silent.)*

I know you're still upset. And you have every right.

...

Will you let me see him?

...

You can't keep him from me. C'mon.

...

JULIA. He belongs here.

REINA. He belongs with me.

JULIA. His whole life is here. Why would you want to take / him from that?

REINA. Because I've built a home for us in the States now. But it doesn't feel like home without him in it. Do you understand?

JULIA. Do I understand? I know very well what it's like to not have your child in the home you've built. To feel like they grew up without you being a part of their life. Yeah, I know that feeling well.

> *(**REINA** is silent.)*

REINA. Look, I have worked to the bone to / get here –

JULIA. YOU LEFT FOR TEN YEARS.

>   *(Silence.)*

Ten Years.

I raised your son.

>   *(Silence.)*

I was the one who made sure he wasn't one of the kids that they pulled out of buses and cars, away from churches and put guns in their hands. I was a wreck every time he wasn't in my sight.

REINA. I was worried sick too. I felt terrible that I couldn't be here. But I felt worse that I couldn't bring him to me. Away from the war.

JULIA. What about me? You think I wasn't worried about you? You think your letters were enough?

REINA. I'm...sorry...I am so. So sorry.

I didn't realize it would take me ten years to prove I was deserving of U.S. citizenship. And it only took me ten seconds in the U.S. to realize I didn't deserve you. You were so hard, but you were raising me to be. Strong. Like you.

...

Thank you.

Will you please forgive me?

Mother?

>   *(**JULIA** is silent.)*

JULIA. *(Sighs.)* I'm not a witch.

REINA. You're not.

>   *(**JULIA** hugs **REINA**. **JULIA** cries.)*

JULIA. *(Wiping tears away.)* You're hungry?

REINA. ...Actually I ate a lot on the plane.

JULIA. You're hungry. I'll make you some *pupusas*.

REINA. Now there's one thing I've definitely missed. Your *pupusas* are the best.

> (**JULIA** *smiles.*)

JULIA. Don't you butter me up. It's working.

> (**REINA** *smiles.*)

REINA. It's nice to be back here.

JULIA. There's no place like home. I'm gonna get Fernando and tell him to come out here.

REINA. Thank you.

> (**JULIA** *exits.* **REINA** *is left alone. She paces.* **THE NARRATOR** *puts his guitar down. The lights shift.* **THE NARRATOR** *becomes a ten-year-old* **FERNANDO**. *He approaches* **REINA**. *She connects with him. He looks to his mother for the first time. There is some distance between the two.)*

Hi.

FERNANDO. Hi.

REINA. Fernando.

FERNANDO. ...

REINA. It's me. Your mom.

FERNANDO. ...

> (**REINA** *is incredibly careful as she approaches* **FERNANDO**.*)*

[MUSIC NO. 23 – BEAUTIFUL BOY (DUET)]

REINA.

LET ME HAVE A LOOK
AT MY BEAUTIFUL BOY.
I'VE MISSED YOUR LITTLE FACE.
I'VE COUNTED THE DAYS
'TIL I'D SEE YOU AND HUG YOU AGAIN
YOU AND I
WERE SO FAR APART
THOUGH I ALWAYS KEPT YOU RIGHT HERE IN MY HEART

FERNANDO.

LET ME HAVE A LOOK
ARE YOU REALLY MY MOM?
I DON'T KNOW YOUR FACE.
WHEN YOU LEFT THIS PLACE,
I COULDN'T EVEN WALK OR RIDE A BIKE
I RECOGNIZE YOUR EYES
FROM A PRETTY OLD PICTURE
HI MOM. IT'S REALLY NICE TO MEET YA.

REINA.

CAN I HAVE A HUG?
AND MAYBE A KISS, OR TWO?
UNLESS YOU DON'T THINK YOU'RE READY TO
IT MIGHT BE A TOUGH THING FOR YOU TO DO.
BUT I'VE COME FROM SO FAR AWAY
FROM THE USA
AND I'VE MISSED YOU SO.
IS THAT SOMEWHERE THAT YOU MIGHT WANT TO GO?

(**FERNANDO** *doesn't answer.*)

COME WITH ME TO A NEW PLACE WE'LL CALL HOME.

(*No answer.*)

PLEASE TELL ME THAT I WON'T LEAVE HERE ALONE!

(*No answer.* **FERNANDO** *stands still.*)

REINA. Fernando?

You don't want to come home with Mommy?

FERNANDO. …

REINA. Honey?

FERNANDO. What about Mama Julia? And my Uncles?

REINA. They can come visit.

FERNANDO. But what about my bike?

REINA. I bought you that bike. I can buy you a brand new one!

(**FERNANDO** *shrugs like "I don't know."*)

REINA. Alright

…

It's alright

(**REINA** *starts to cry.*)

FERNANDO. Are you okay?

REINA. I'm just so happy to see you.

FERNANDO. Okay.

REINA. You should go play.

(**FERNANDO** *starts to turn.* **ADÁN** *comes out of the house with a basketball and bounces it to* **FERNANDO**.)

ADÁN. (*To* **FERNANDO**.) Hey kid, come here.

You know where your mom lives?

(**FERNANDO** *nods no.*)

Your mom lives in Chicago.

(**FERNANDO** *lights up.*)

What else is in Chicago?

FERNANDO. Chicago Bulls!

ADÁN. That's right. The Chicago Bulls. Who's your favorite player?

FERNANDO. Michael Jordan.

ADÁN. That's right! Michael Jordan plays in the same city your mom lives.

(*To* **REINA.**) We've been watching MJ play on television. Kid's obsessed.

REINA. (*To* **FERNANDO.**) I didn't know you liked the Bulls! I've seen where they play!

FERNANDO. Nuh-uh!

REINA. Yes!

ADÁN. Isn't that crazy?

(**FERNANDO** *nods yes.*)

FERNANDO. Could I see them?

ADÁN. *Puchica!*

Good luck getting those tickets sis!

Hey listen, I gotta go run to get *chicharrón* for Mom's feast. (*To* **FERNANDO.**) You watch her okay? She's a troublemaker like you!

(**FERNANDO** *does a thumbs up.* **ADÁN** *kisses* **REINA** *on the cheek and exits.*)

FERNANDO. Have you met Michael Jordan?

REINA. I haven't. But I've seen him play on TV. Like you. And he's pretty good.

FERNANDO. He's the best.

REINA. I like how he sticks his tongue out when he shoots like this. *(She demonstrates.)*

FERNANDO. *(Laughing.)* Yeah!

(They both do it and laugh.)

REINA. And you know what? I can get you a pair of his shoes. So, you can be just like him.

FERNANDO. Really?

REINA. Yes. Would you like that?

FERNANDO. A pair of Air Jordans?

REINA. Yes. We'll be broke for a little bit, but for you, honey, it's worth it. And I'll take you to school every day. And I can make you dinner every night. And we'll be...together.

*(**REINA** offers her hand.)*

FERNANDO. Okay.

REINA. ...Okay you'll come?

*(**FERNANDO** nods yes.)*

FERNANDO. Can we go inside and eat first though?

REINA. *(She laughs.)* Of course. Come on.

(Sound of an airplane flying overhead.)

[MUSIC NO. 24 – BEAUTIFUL BOY (UNDERSCORE)]

*(**REINA** hands **FERNANDO** a shoebox. Inside is a pair of bright red Air Jordans.* **FERNANDO** *opens them. His face lights up as he puts them on. Lights shift.)*

---

* A license to produce *SOMEWHERE OVER THE BORDER* does not include a license to publicly display any branded logos or trademarked images. Licensees must acquire rights for any logos and/or images or create their own.

REINA & FERNANDO.
YOU AND I
WILL BE TOGETHER
IN ANOTHER PLACE THAT'S BETTER FOR US
JUST YOU AND ME.

(Lights shift.)

Scene Twenty-One

Epilogue

[MUSIC NO. 25 – EVERYDAY TOWNS (REPRISE)]

THE NARRATOR/FERNANDO.
THERE ARE TOWNS, LIKE MANY, MANY OTHER TOWNS
DIFF'RENT BUT SIMILAR TOWNS IN MANY OTHER
COUNTRIES,

COMPANY EXCEPT REINA.
ALL ACROSS THE EARTH
WITH PEOPLE WHO GO 'BOUT THEIR DAYS
TRYIN' TO GIVE THEIR OWN LIFE SOME SORT OF WORTH

THE NARRATOR/FERNANDO.
MAKIN' THE BEST OF THE BEST WITH WHAT THEY GOT
TOWNS WITH FORGOTTEN PEOPLE,
WHO LIVE WHETHER THEY HAVE THE MEANS OR NOT.

COMPANY EXCEPT REINA.
WORKING TO LIVE OR LIVING TO MAKE THEIR DREAMS
COME TRUE
THE WORLD IS FILLED WITH DREAMERS, DREAMERS LIKE
ME AND YOU.
DREAMERS LIKE ME AND YOU. DREAMERS LIKE ME AND
YOU.

THE NARRATOR/FERNANDO.
EV'RYDAY DREAMERS. IN EV'RYDAY TOWNS.
WITH COMMON EV'RYDAY PEOPLE
OUT THERE MAKING THEIR ROUNDS.

COMPANY.
EV'RYDAY TOWNS WITH EV'RYDAY FOLK
EV'RYDAY DREAMERS WITH STORIES THAT MUST BE TOLD.

THE NARRATOR/FERNANDO. This world is filled with stories.

SILVANO. Famous stories

ADÁN. Forgotten stories

JULIA. Tragic stories

LEONA. And joyful stories.

REINA. Stories that honor the journey

COMPANY EXCEPT REINA. And the people who made it so.

THE NARRATOR/FERNANDO. This is the story of a mother

REINA. And her son.

THE NARRATOR/FERNANDO. Out of so many stories of everyday people

REINA. From everyday towns,

THE NARRATOR/FERNANDO & REINA.

This.

Is just one.

> *(***THE NARRATOR/FERNANDO*** clicks his heels together.)*

> *(Blackout.)*

End of Play

[MUSIC NO. 26 – BOWS & EXIT MUSIC]